"You in ...
he sai ...

"I've never met a woman so challenging and direct."

"And you don't like it, do you?" Ally exclaimed. "No doubt about it, you've got a little problem there."

"And you've got a big one if you won't admit at least one man as your master. Men do rule the earth, Alison. And you know why? It's our role. It's what nature equipped us for."

A current of hostility and excitement was flowing between them, making her nervous behind her cloak of defiance.

"Certainly, only men are intoxicated with power," she said. "You've been trying to repress me from the moment we met."

He laughed outright. "I don't find too much aggression convenient in my lady friends! Don't think for a moment I'll put up with it in you!"

Margaret Way takes great pleasure in her work and works hard at her pleasure. She enjoys tearing off to the beach with her family on weekends, loves haunting galleries and auctions and is completely given over to French champagne "for every possible joyous occasion." Her home, perched high on a hill overlooking Brisbane, Australia, is her haven. She started writing when her son was a baby, and now she finds there is no better way to spend her time.

Books by Margaret Way

Don't miss any of our special offers. Write to us at the following address for information on our newest releases.

Harlequin Reader Service
901 Fuhrmann Blvd., P.O. Box 1397, Buffalo, NY 14240
Canadian address: P.O. Box 603,
Fort Erie, Ont. L2A 5X3

Mowana Magic

Margaret Way

Harlequin Books

TORONTO • NEW YORK • LONDON
AMSTERDAM • PARIS • SYDNEY • HAMBURG
STOCKHOLM • ATHENS • TOKYO • MILAN

Original hardcover edition published in 1988
by Mills & Boon Limited

ISBN 0-373-02976-4

Harlequin Romance first edition April 1989

CHAPTER ONE

EVEN at a distance, the man striding across the tarmac had such a diamond-hard *toughness*, Ally stumbled away from the plate-glass window and collapsed into a bucket chair.

Impossible. Simply *impossible*. She had to be wrong.

Ever the optimist, she gained strength through hope. She pushed up and peered out.

The man raised his arm and waved at her.

Dear God! Ally spun back against the wall, rearing her burnished head like a filly about to bolt.

Hadn't she always known in her heart that she would see him again? Some time. Somewhere. Lurid images flashed into her mind. Images that even now made her whole body convulse with shame and anger. Whatever she had done then, she had always got herself into a tangle.

A blast from the swivelling wall-fan picked up her long, lustrous hair and blew it across her face. She could *still* have a chance! She was moreover, *hopeful* . Two years ago, she hadn't been the glamorous old Ally she was today. She hadn't even begun her phenomenal move to success. She'd been two stone heavier, for one thing, with undeniably lush curves. Her now legendary curling mane had grown from an uncontrollable marmalade sunburst, and her always flushed, chubby cheeks had been pared down to the bone.

The young Ally had virtually disappeared. She had been replaced by the highly professional, top-fashion Allegra. In appearances, anyway. She continued to be Ally inside, which meant a warm, impulsive, good old-fashioned girl. The difficulty was to prove it, especially with a magnificent body.

That particular shocking episode had been her only encounter with him. *Senseless little baggage* he had called her, which showed how badly he had misjudged her. She was all of five foot ten in her stockinged feet.

Of course, he wouldn't know her. Zoe had seen to that. In no way had she resembled the superstar the Zoe Campbell Modelling Agency had worked long and hard to make her. She herself had endured and won out with daily workouts and a highly nutritious diet that tasted mostly like crushed beetles. The agency walls were lined with huge blow-ups of her face and lithe body. True to the fairy-godmother tradition, Zoe had taken Ally over and remade her from scratch. It was largely due to Zoe that Ally now spoke with what she called her posh accent. The young Ally, with her lazy country drawl overlaid by an inherited accent, had never ignored good advice. She had rushed out and enrolled in speech and singing lessons around the clock, and just in case her education became too trivialised she achieved academic qualifications hitherto denied her through night-school.

'Our Ally is destined for the very top!' her darling little mum was fond of telling everyone within earshot, to which her scatchy, stiff-necked father invariably replied, 'There's a limit to what we battlers can do.' Ally, however, was a very practical and steadfast girl. She was also ambitious. Her instinct was to go for it. And her instinct had paid off.

Even now. Especially now. The terminal doors opened and the man walked in. So darkly magnificent, so menacing, that Ally felt her mouth go dry. So strong was his impact, she stood absolutely still, like a creature of the wild, frozen in fright. Where were her theories about the power of positive thought? Be bold, be resolute, she ordered her quaking limbs. He might not recognise her at all. Apart from her changed looks, much depended on dressing. The young Ally, in a home-made party dress, was a hoyden compared to now. Her job and a healthy ego demanded she look beautifully groomed at all times, and her three-piece outfit, ginger linen jacket and slacks worn with a vibrantly patterned pure silk shirt, bore a world-famous designer label. The party dress, she remembered to her sorrow, had come apart at the seams, albeit with excessive strain. She still thought of it as her bodice-ripper.

With a tremendous effort she freed herself from a male power that almost totally demoralised her. She moved forwards in her tawny elegance, flashing him her marvellously sunny smile; all wide, luscious mouth and even, pearly teeth. She was only vulnerable if she blushed, stammered, or couldn't meet his amazing eyes.

'Mr Lancaster!' As proof of her courage, she placed herself directly before him, staring up into his startling eyes. Staring upwards was in itself an unusual experience. Eight times out of ten her gaze was down-bent.

He didn't speak for a moment, his expression mid-way between pleasant and acutely sharp, his glittering eyes brilliant as spotlights on her upturned face. 'Why, Miss Allen,' he said finally, admiring, but a long way from besotted. 'Allegra, may I?'

'Why, of course you may!' Sheer relief made her bat her velvety brown lashes. 'We finally meet.'

Rock-crystal eyes glinted, only change of expression.

'A pity, you must have been a spectacular school-girl.'

'I'm used to amusement.'

'Never! I think there's a wonderful joy in being tall.'

'You would!' she said soulfully, her golden-brown eyes skimming his six-foot-four frame. 'No one would dare ask *you* how the weather was up there.'

The disturbingly attractive mouth quirked in a smile. 'Speaking of which, we'd better get going. We've had a few electrical storms of late, and I'd like to give you a nice ride.'

'I wouldn't miss it for the world,' she enthused. 'I was in

Fiji last week on location, now the great Outback!' Though she was prickly with a high intensity, she also felt elation. He was all kinds of a great guy, but he lost out on perception. Most men weren't as observant as they fondly imagined. What a blessing!

'Where's your luggage?' He favoured her with another of his glinting looks. Why, the man's eyes were pure silver!

'I do hope I haven't brought too much.' She gestured with an elegant, enamel tipped hand.

'We can always put another room on.' He muttered a bit at the four pieces, but scooped them up neatly, shaking his head at a young attendant who ran forward with a trolley.

'Tell me about Sacha. Please.' She actually had to skip along the tarmac, heading towards his splendid winged chariot.

'She's feeling a little sad these days, as you probably know.'

'Not everybody enjoys falling in love,' she commented sagely.

'She's not in love.' He halted so abruptly, Ally too came to a frantic stop.

'Well . . . ' She put her head on the side, staring up at him thoughtfully. What a personage! There was something so very implacable about him. A man to hold in awe.

'The guy is clever, I grant you. It's practically impossible to tell him from the real thing, but I've seen the same game played before. I was absolutely livid when I realised what he was up to.'

'Did smoke come out of your ears?'

'It sure as hell did,' he retorted tightly. 'Panic all round.' He walked to the front of the Beech Baron and stored the luggage in the nose-locker. 'Scatty little things like Sacha always need protection.'

'Isn't scatty a bit harsh?' She gave him a rueful smile.

'Can you give me another word?'

Ally tried to think of one. 'As a matter of fact, no.' Sacha was downright dotty.

'You two must have a lot in common.'

The thrust shocked her. 'That's right, and I love it!' Although she kept the challenging smile on her face, Ally felt her heart rock.

'Yes, ma'am, I know trouble when I see it.'

'Whatever are you talking about? She looked up at him blithely.

'You're not here for some mischief?'

'I'm devastated, Mr Lancaster,' Ally answered promply. 'I'm here at the invitation of a friend!'

'You don't want to turn and bolt?'

'Probably another woman would, but not me.'

He nodded his handsome, dark head abruptly. 'You haven't changed much.'

She took a deep breath. 'You surprise me. This is the first time I've met you.'

'Really?' One heavy, black eyebrow shot up and he gave her a killing look. 'I thought it was at a party.'

'Well, I'll be damned,' she said lamely.

'Still want to come along?' His hand fell heavily on her shoulder.

'Hey, that's hurting.'

'Sorry.' He took his hand away deliberately. 'I'm giving you time to consider your decision.'

'I'm a different girl, you know. I mean, I'm the same but you misjudged the whole situation.'

The diamond-hard gaze narrowed. 'I beg you if you're coming to be very, very careful out here.'

'Right.' She swallowed, her long, creamy throat rippling.

'I don't know why, but losing those bouncy curves has made you even sexier,' he said slowly.

'I never figured I bounced!' she retorted sharply.

'You did. I never saw anyone bounce like that in my entire

life.'

'Your big problem is you like to play judge and jury,' she responded hotly, vivid colouring coming to the fore.

'You're still protesting you're innocent?'

She sighed deeply, but it came out as a voluptuous exhalation. 'I guess you'll never believe me.'

'I think you ought to know Prentice came to talk to me after,' he told her in amused contempt.

'*No!*' She was shocked and she looked it.

'Just between us boys.' The smile on the sculptured mouth didn't reach the frosty eyes.

'Is there any way you'll listen to my side of the story?' she asked him.

'What do you think?' He showed her where to climb to the pilot's door by a single step behind the wing.

'I think not. These days I'm pretty street smart.'

'You were then.' He cast an insufferable glance over her face and slender neck.

'Does he still crack his knuckles?'

'I wouldn't know,' he shrugged carelessly. 'I don't really deal with shockers.'

'So why did you speak to him?' She tilted her head back, disconcerted by the strange thrum in her blood.

'My dear girl, he came to me,' he drawled sardonically. 'He described his relationship with you, and what a hint of scandal would do to his career. He never paid any attention to his wife.'

'Look, why don't we change the subject?' Ally suggested wryly. 'You just admitted Prentice was a shocker, but you preferred to believe him rather than me. That's OK. Men stick together. Something else I've learned. I can't remake the world.' For the time being, anyway. She felt completely zonked out.

*   *   *

Ally had been living in the city for just under a year, sharing a flat with two girlfriends and working at her latest job as one of the receptionists with a firm of public relations consultants dealing with corporate communications and special projects. She had originally applied as a Girl Friday, which meant a general dogsbody, but obviously her flouncing, bouncing whatever had fallen on the right eyes. Within a month she had been promoted to receptionist, even at a time when, homesick, she had been gaining weight. From that very moment business picked up. Clients didn't ring, they came to call. To a country girl it was a breeze to smile and be pleasant, but as one of the senior receptionists said sourly, 'How can we cope with such competition?'

Roger Prentice, a property investor by profession, and a man with political aspirations, was a frequent visitor to the office, when once they had rarely seen him. The same senior receptionist had told her the guileless Ally he was planning to ask her out but Ally put her bright head on one side, clearly not believing a word of it. Not only was Mr Prentice married with children, but he was doddery by her standards. When he finally did ask her out, Ally had almost fallen sideways.

'That guy's bad news,' the senior receptionist told her more kindly. 'How about this for a joke? You look the definitive *femme fatale* and you're really a nice girl.'

'Absolutely. I give my word.' Ally's equanimity was shaken.

Nevertheless, it was judged politic for a good many of the firm to attend Roger Prentice's fund-raisings. Mostly it had been good fun. Plenty to eat and drink—Ally had not yet learned about diets; splendid locales—Prentice was a wealthy man; and the crowds were very interesting, up-market people.

Ally, being Ally, drew men like bees. Unlike her many friends, she wasn't sexually active. Quite the contrary. She loved being kissed tenderly, she loved talking on the phone, but she was her mother's daughter, and her mother had taught her that her body was sacred and special. Ally wanted to be loved passionately, which was not very unusual: what *was* unusual was her strict adherence to her principles. On no account would she fall from grace. She did in time, but that came with age.

When Prentice finally won his seat, he threw a big party and, without considering her judgement, Ally went along. Even now the memory woke her up in a cold sweat. The party was well under way before Prentice decided on a course of action that made both of them look senseless and cheap. Moreover, it was a grave offence, because Mrs Prentice was the hostess on her own premises.

'You little tease!' Prentice had cried wolfishly.

'Not me. You're crazy!'

'Crazy, eh?' Pushing her into what was presumably his inner sanctum, because his photographs lined the walls, he'd given a maddened laugh. 'You don't know what you make me feel.' He had started pawing her right away. 'I can make everything in life better for you.'

'If you think that, you're bonkers.' Ally had looked back at him, speechless.

'Sleep with me.' Though he barely came up to her chin, he'd grasped her powerfully.

'*Mr Prentice!*' Ally had cried a warning, but the experience of clasping her warm body in his arms had sent his libido soaring. It was no exaggeration to say they'd wrestled around the room; indeed, it looked as though someone had made up a new dance! A platter of salted macadamias had tipped over, then a glass of beer. Despite her superior height, Ally had been struggling to survive. The party dress she had been so proud of, white, splashed in Picasso colours—she'd had a penchant for brilliance in those days—had burst the seams of it figure-hugging bodice, affording a lavish display of her creamy breasts and sloping shoulders. Ally had had no fear of being raped, the place had been too crowded, but she had known she couldn't handle much more. Did a rising politician hold an orgy in his own home? Things she had never dreamt of?

Just as Ally had been considering calamitous action and a whole lot of publicity, her saviour had arrived at the door—a man who, intent only on making a phone call, had acted as though he had been witness to some kind of bash. He'd looked so big and dangerous, Prentice had instantly turned into a wimp.

In the end, it had been Ally who'd felt like telling her saviour to get lost. His words had been so cutting, she had broken out in weals. He had massacred them with his tongue, said things even Ally couldn't recall. Prentice somehow came out the disgusting victim, and she the houri who danced around inciting decent men madness. Apparently Mrs Prentice was some kind of relative. Finally, with Roger Prentice stripped of all esteem, the stranger had escorted Ally out by the garden door to her decorated Beetle, got her seated behind the wheel and advised her in unvarnished tones to go home. He had come on just too strong, even if he had taught her a lot. Her eardrums had throbbed. The only thing he hadn't called her was a giraffe. And he remembered. Several years on, he still *remembered*!

'You're really lost in thought,' said Kiall Lancaster above the quiet drone of the twin engines.

'I thought I had succeeded in putting my past behind me.' They were airborne, but Ally was conscious of little but his nearness.

'Never say that to me.'

'Doesn't it trouble you to be so judgemental?'

'What troubles me is leaving you and Sacha loose together. Where did you meet my little half-sister, anyway?'

'I do occasionally mix with the idle rich,' she quipped

jauntily.

'I'll bet that's right. How come you haven't found yourself a rich husband? Surely that was the idea.'

'Actually, I refused an offer of marriage about a month ago,' she smirked prettily.

'Didn't think he'd survive the ceremony? Lew Grasswell, wasn't it?'

'*Sir* Lewis, yes.'

'Everything perfect except his age?'

'Sir Lewis is a gentleman,' Ally returned severely.

'Well, he's what, sixty-seven or eight? That might have *something* to do with it.'

'Anyway, how did you know?' she challenged him, her high cheekbones catching fire.

'Sacha told us all about it. You wrote her one of your screamingly funny letters, remember?'

'She didn't show it to you, did she?'

'You're lucky, she didn't.'

'There was nothing in it that couldn't have been read by a child. Important men don't give a damn if they don't look good. They don't even care if they're rising ninety. They genuinely believe any woman would be glad to catch them.'

'And aren't they?'

'The man to interest me will have to have more than a hefty bank balance.'

He laughed.

'You'd better believe it,' Ally said.

'Don't look at *me*.' He smiled mockingly. 'I'm all tied up.'

'Don't say you got married in the last month?' She opened her eyes wide.

'I meant the station,' he said smoothly. 'Mowana is my life.'

'I've never seen an outback station before.'

'I should say that they haven't seen anyone so exotic.'

'Exotic, *me*?'

'It nearly threw me for a loop when I saw you through the terminal window.'

'Gosh, you're quite a character. I would have thought I'd changed a lot.'

'What does a lioness use for a disguise? Now, what about Sacha? How did you meet her?'

'Would you believe a street march?'

'No.'

'Actually, she did a course at my modelling agency. A sort of discover-your-potential. I took some of the courses. It helped supplement my income. I was a little older. Sacha took to me right away. She's such a bubbly creature.'

'Don't let the big blue eyes fool you,' he warned. 'She's one single-minded little lady. What Sacha wants, Sacha has to have. Keeping her out of trouble had been a major commitment.'

'You don't think you should loosen up?' Ally looked at him through her lashes.

'In no way whatsoever. It might speed things up if I tell you I'm the law on Mowana. I must be obeyed.'

Of course, Sacha had told her he was a tyrant. It had always been that way. Sacha's mother, his stepmother, never thought to question him, apparently. In fact, she was said to wave incense at his feet. A man who looked like that was bound to be a holy terror with the ladies, Ally found herself thinking. In a way that really goaded her, he was a stunning-looking man.

'Just take a look down there,' she said presently, her mind transfixed by the wild immensity. 'Isn't it magnificent?'

'It is now,' he agreed, his voice deepened with feeling. 'We've been blessed with rain. In good times, the promised land, in drought a positive hell. You look English—are you? That rare skin.'

'My parents emigrated when I was two,' she told him. 'My mother was born in the Scottish Highlands, little Ally

MacGregor. She still speaks with a marvellous soft accent. My father hailed from Birmingham, and Birmingham boys don't cry.'

'So you have your mother's colouring, right?' He turned his head to search her tawny eyes.

She nodded. 'My mother is the prettiest woman you can imagine. So soft and sweet and gentle. A perfect delight. I can never understand how she and my father got together. I suppose love does strange things. Believe it or not, I was ruled with a rod of iron.'

'So, naturally, when you got the chance you broke out,' he rejoined suavely.

'That meant a lot to you, didn't it, seeing me grapple with that tipsy rabbit? I suppose it was because you knew the hostess.'

'Not just know her. There's a family connection.'

'So you go into a primal war-dance every time the relatives play up at parties?'

'Not really,' he said derisively. 'You were just so lush, I couldn't take it. It was like seeing a magnificent Rubens in the wrong hands.'

'Rubens? Oh, God,' she said despairingly, 'I have never in my entire life been fat.'

The flash in his eyes was like the sun reflected on ice. 'Did I say fat? I said lush, as in luscious. A peach. A swelling, flowering, high-coloured fruit of the earth. Opulent is another word that comes to mind. In a way, it's barbarous that you lost all that weight. A lot of men apart from Prentice must have found it exciting.'

Ally made a strangled noise in her throat. 'I'd like to relieve your mind, but they seem to find it more exciting now I've taken it off.'

'Really?' His voice was lazy but his eyes were not. 'Too much adoration couldn't be good for you. I know you've probably heard it before, but the goddess of the hunt couldn't have looked much different.'

Ally sat up straight, narrowing her eyes on this insolent man. 'Is this the way you greet all Sacha's friends?'

'Sacha's friends are hard to find,' pointed out Kiall Lancaster drily. 'Girlfriends, that is. That's between you and me, of course. I think she's invited you to distract me.'

Ally looked at him with fine disdain. 'How melodramatic, and how scary! Why, it's positively insane.'

'Is it?' His eyes shimmered over her, and for a fraction of a second Ally's guarded heart quivered in her breast. 'If I only had a little time . . . '

'You work seven days a week?' She found refuge in flippancy, keeping her voice soft and sexy.

'Flirt if you feel like it,' he encouraged her. 'I'll play along.'

She nodded. 'I took you for a closet playboy all along. Sacha didn't talk much about her family, apart from saying they were landed gentry and very rich.'

'Is that why you investigated?'

'Your ego is as big as your homestead, Mr Lancaster. I'm one of those highly paid working girls. My own woman.'

'Good,' he clipped approvingly, devilish dancing lights in his eyes. 'I like independence in anything. Horses. Women. But surely you want your dazzling career to lead to something bigger?'

'Certainly not a lousy marriage,' she retorted snappily. 'I'm waiting until true love comes along.'

'Oh, hell, yes. True love. You believe in it?'

She thought for a full minute. 'Yes,' she said finally.

Unexpectedly, he made a sound that was almost a sigh. 'You may be right. Your little file might not tell you my mother left Mowana when I was just a child. Six, to be exact.'

'Never!' declared Ally, shocked. 'You must have been a gorgeous little boy.'

A hard light flared into his eyes. 'I was brought up to believe marrying a beautiful woman was a crime.'

'That was your father's pain and anger,' she protested, seeing him very vividly as a child, with coal-black curls clinging to a beautifully shaped head, and with big, luminous eyes.

'Of course.' There was a brooding look on his dark, stormy features. 'Amazingly, however, he married again. Sacha's mother. She had to pay for all that his power and position could do for her. My father was a legendary hard man. The casual observer might have called him a tyrant. You'll like Susan. She's a very nice woman. As vulnerable as Sacha's tough.'

'You're tough yourself,' she told him with tart honesty. 'In fact, you look so tough its's staggering.'

'Then watch out, Allegra,' he warned her, staring right into her eyes. 'You obviously need a firm hand, and you could get it.'

CHAPTER TWO

FROM the air, the Lancaster homestead, surrounded by its many outbuildings, resembled a medieval fortress floating in the middle of a great moat.

'Oh, how marvellous, how romantic!' Ally cried, enchanted, her eyes on the enormous area of red roofing and the broad silver lagoon that completely encircled the compound. 'There must be some way I can get a place like this if I work at it.'

'If you intend to work on *me,* let me know,' Kiall Lancaster warned her.

'No, seriously,' she said, her eyes gleaming topaz, 'this is *magic!*'

'*I* think so.' He smiled at her for the first time without mockery, but with great charm. 'My family have been extremely fortunate to hold on to it all this time. My great-great-grandparents arrived here in the 1840s, after travelling up from New South Wales. Charles Lancaster, from all accounts, was a most remarkable and sophisticated man. He left a privileged life back in England to build up his own empire. He was so successful, at one time our family controlled millions of acres of land. If you can imagine what it was like back then, then you'll know just how tough empire builders had to be. We're right on Capricorn, so all this was uncharted jungle. As well as that, the natives weren't docile, they were pretty warlike. Provisions had to come in on lumbering bullock-drays with enough to last maybe for a couple of years.'

'I'll bet the lady of the house wasn't laughing.'

'Actually,' he turned to glance at her, 'Charles Lancaster had three wives.'

'All at the same time?'

'It was for him to decide.' His eyes gleamed. 'Out here in those days he must have been a law unto himself. But no, I'm happy to tell you, one at a time.'

'So who left him?'

'One by one they died.'

'My God, there must have been a lot of weeping.'

'There must have been. Women died, children died. Pioneers took on a punishing venture.'

'So the toughness is bred into you?'

'The will to survive.'

She turned away from that handsome, relentless profile. 'The homestead looks huge.'

'I suppose it is,' he agreed casually. 'Wings have been added over the years, guest bungalows. We have a lot of visitors, from here and overseas, even the Royals from the Duke of Windsor's time, when he was Prince of Wales. My grandparents were very sociable. My father more or less turned into a recluse after my mother left him.'

'That must have ben a great tragedy. For him and for you.'

'It was cruel.'

It was said with such harshness that tears came into Ally's eyes. 'Weren't things better when Susan and then your little half-sister arrived?'

'Difficult to answer. As a man, I realised how much Susan tried to comfort me, but I wanted my own mother. Sacha was a playful little thing, but there's no question she was tremendously spoiled. By her mother, that is. My father was indifferent to a girl child. Sons he would have driven into the ground. And sons he wanted. At the very least, four. Sadly for Susan, she couldn't breed sons. She never did get over Sacha's difficult birth. In the old days, I'm sure my father would have simply sent her away and taken a stronger mate, but the Lancasters are too well known in this modern world. Susan stayed and she paid.'

'I gather your father was a hard, bitter man.'

'I've said the same thing myself occasionally.'

'And he died. Sacha told me.'

'Suicide is a better word.'

'Surely not?' Ally blinked.

'He flew from Mowana to the coast when a cyclone warning was posted. He never made it. We flew over the very spot he came down in. Devil's Peak. A place to be avoided from time immemorial. According to aboriginal legend it's the guardian of the great spirit that slumbers at its feet, another fantastic rock formation. My father knew what he was doing. He always knew what he was doing. The only thing that ever got away from him was my mother.'

'She must have been one spunky lady.'

'To leave a child?' His silver eyes raked her.

'From the sound of things she mightn't have had much choice.'

'There's always a choice,' he said without anger, but very firmly. 'Do you ride?'

'Do I what?' asked Ally blithely.

'You do?' He gave her a straight, no-nonsense look.

'Trains and buses. Horses are new to me. I'm fascinated by their big teeth.'

Kiall Lancaster gave a short laugh. 'I'll teach you to ride, if I don't teach you anything else. We'll find you a horse so your legs don't reach the ground.'

'Go ahead,' Ally snorted. 'You won't get a rise out of me. I've been listening to little quips since childhood. They follow me around.'

'I'll buy that,' he smiled. 'Plus legions of admirers. That hair of yours, the colour's real?'

'As real as the cleft in your chin.'

'I didn't think you got it from a bottle. I can understand why you're a model. Looks like your hair would naturally influence your choice of job.'

'The pay's good. I meet a lot of people. See a lot of places. As of now, Mowana had put everything else in the shade. How come Sacha doesn't talk about it and talk about it? It's magnificent!'

'Sacha can't take too much time on the station,' Kiall told her.

'I guess I'm just a country girl,' Ally sighed.

'Are you? You don't look like a country anything.'

'Heredity must mean something. I'm my mother's daughter, and she loves the land with a passion. My father was a reluctant farmer, but my mother couldn't breathe in the city. Now, neither would ever think of living any place else. At least I'll be able to milk your cows.'

'Thanks, but I can't ask you.' He released the landing-gear as they approached the downward leg.

'Oh, we're going down,' she remarked with interest.

'It's necessary if we want to land.'

'Will Sacha be there?'

'Of course. We've got an extra visitor, by the look of it. See that single-engined Cessna? That's a long-time friend of ours come to get a line on Sacha's pal.'

'Splendid,' Ally nodded. 'What's his name?'

'*Her* name,' he corrected drily. 'You've heard of, or read about, the Fulbrooks?'

'I enjoy reading, but not so far.'

'Joshua Fulbrook?'

'Ah, yes.' Ally positively beamed at him. 'Sir Joshua is a household name.'

'Karen is his granddaughter. The Fulbrooks are big landowners.'

'Count on it if you want to fly your own plane.' Ally quipped drily.

He ignored her. 'Fulbrook Park is to the south-west of us, our nearest neighbour.'

'Am I to assume this Karen is very attached to you?'

He glanced at her briefly. 'I'm out of the habit of wondering.'

'About women?' She gave him a slow, curving smile.

'Be a good girl and tighten that seat-belt,' he cautioned her. 'It's moments before we touch down. We can leave the interrogation to another time.'

'Ally, Ally, darling!' Sacha cried. She sounded so genuinely thrilled to see her, Ally's heart melted with warmth.

'Lovely to see you!' The two girls embraced.

'Hey, big brother,' Sacha reached back to give Kiall Lancaster a hug, 'thanks a lot.'

'Your "gorgeous friend Ally" surpassed even my expectations,' he informed Sacha drily.

'Thank you.' Hastily, Ally gave him a brilliant smile. He might mention that they had met before, in which case she might want to hide. But he turned away to greet someone: a young woman dressed in an ivory silk shirt and moleskins.

'Ah, Karen, when did you arrive?'

She was very striking indeed: glossy, dark hair cut in a crisp but feminine short style, and huge dark eyes set at a faint slant. It had to be mentioned that she was petite. Five-foot three at the most, but so slim, and the bearing so confident, even arrogant, lack of height was of no importance.

To Ally's interested eyes, she seemed to coil herself against Kiall Lancaster's muscular chest so that it was obligatory for him to bend that high-mettled head and brush his lips against her sun-kissed cheek.

Karen Fulbrook looked like serious business.

'Oh, Ally, let me introduce you,' Sacha cried boldly, almost breaking up the embrace. 'This is our dear friend Karen

Fulbrook. Karen's family own the adjoining station. Karen,' Sacha put her hand on Ally's arm and pressed her forward. 'meet Allegra Allen.'

'How do you do?' Ally gave her lovely, bright smile, instantly dubbing Miss Fulbrook trouble as their glances clashed.

'How are you, Miss Allen?' Karen returned severely, appearing not to notice Ally's half-way hovering hand. 'Of course, I've seen photographs of you in various magazines. Fabulous, I must say, but you must hate being so tall.'

'The truth,' Ally admitted, 'but I can't complain.'

'You sure as hell can't.' Unexpectedly, Kiall Lancaster lifted a long, thick strand of her hair and wound it around his lean, long-fingered hand.

'You can say that again,' Sacha seconded, laughing. 'Let's go up to the house. I can't wait to show you around, Ally. Oh, this is so exciting! Coming with us, Kiall?'

'Regrettably, no.'

'Can't you make an exception?'

He shook his head. 'I'll see you at dinner.'

'You work too hard,' Karen crooned at him.

'How else do things get done?'

For a moment Ally watched, fascinated, as those big, dark eyes of Karen's devoured him. Not that he really wasn't something, his tall, rangy body leaning negligently against the plane's fusilage: wide shoulders, narrow hips, his startling eyes in contrast to hair as black as a crow's wing, and sun-coppered skin.

'You're coming with us, aren't you, Karen?' Sacha asked with a trace of sarcasm.

'Go head,' Karen ordered without turning her head. 'I have an important message for Kiall from my father.'

'She has an important message for Kiall from her father,' Sacha hissed as she started the engine of the waiting Range

Rover. 'Couldn't take long to say it. Won't you please marry my daughter?'

'Like that, is it?' Ally couldn't resist turning her head and giving Kiall and Karen a little wave.

'Karen could have been married a dozen times, but she won't settle for anyone less than Kiall. She'd mad about him. Sometimes I think mad enough to commit a crime.'

'Wow! I hope the competition have their life insurance paid up.'

'I reckon Karen's frightened at least five girls off. Maybe six, and I'm not exaggerating.'

'Good grief!' Ally looked at her friend, startled. 'It can't be dull around here.'

'Why do you think I split so often? Poor old Mum!' Sacha's blonde, pert features softened. 'Karen treats her like a nothing in her own home. It's a dreadful thing to see. Karen, the landed gentry, and Mum, masquerading as the real thing. No one, but no one, had forgotten the first Mrs Lancaster, Kiall's mother. It only takes a careless word to be spoken and all the old wounds open up.'

Ally was attending to Sacha so closely that she was only marginally aware of the timeless grandeur around: lush vegetation, deep permanent water, the jagged, inky-blue line of ranges rising sheer out of the vast savannahs. Years wouldn't be time enough to take it in.

'But surely so much time has passed . . . ' Ally said as the thought struck her.

'Who was it said the past is never past, it's right now?'

'I've read it of course, but I can't come up with a name. If Kiall's mother left when he was only *six* . . . '

'He told you?' Sacha interrupted, so surprised that her voice rose to a squeak.

'Well, yes.'

'Feel honoured, dear girl. Kiall never mentions his mother

to anyone.'

'She's still alive?' Ally asked surreptitiously, as though Kiall might be right behind her.

'You've heard of the Ewings, haven't you?'

'Only, I fear, as in Dallas.'

'That's what I mean.' Sacha swept the Range Rover around a bend, and a thousand multi-coloured parrots shot out of the sentinel rows of willowy, grey-green trees. 'Adele married a Texan rancher with even more money than my father. Things happen in strange ways. Salinger came to Mowana for the Arabian sales. All the Lancasters love horses. Our stud is the best. I don't think you'd believe the price an American rancher paid for our leading stallion only a few months ago. Anyway, whatever Salinger promised her, Adele decided to go.'

'It couldn't have been money,' Ally said, drinking in Mowana's magnificence.

'No, it wasn't money,' Sacha agreed in a low voice. 'Like most women, Adele needed love and attention. Don't try to visualise my father. By any standards, he was a harsh man.'

'Then the real tragedy was Kiall. It must be frightful for a small child to lose his mother. All the more dreadful if the remaining parent isn't kind and loving.'

'Oh, Dad loved Kiall all right,' Sacha answered, almost bleakly. 'He just couldn't show it, or somehow feared to. He paid no attention to me. I was a sort of wind-up toy, a Barbie doll. No real looks, no brains. Hell, I can't even ride a horse properly, and that, for a Lancaster, is shocking.'

'So what about Leon?' Ally decided to change to a less hurtful subject.

'I received a letter only yesterday—smuggled in. Oh, Ally, he *adores* me! Kiall thinks it's the money. He wants me to promise I'll wait, but I'll be twenty-one in a month's time. All I have is an allowance, and a trust fund when I marry. Dad saw to that. Kiall controls everything. Leon loves me because

I'm me, not because one day I'll have money.'

'So why is convincing your brother hard work?'

'You haven't seen Leon,' Sacha said wryly. 'He's the very opposite to Kiall. He's an art dealer, that's how we met him. He and a restorer came to give their advice about Mowana's art collection. It's fairly extensive. The family have been collectors since the early days. The first Charles Lancaster had a good many pictures sent out from England. Some he inherited, and many he bought. I know you'll be suitably impressed. You love beautiful things. Adele was the one who bought Australian paintings. Before that, all the paintings had been European. It's quite a job looking after the collection, and Leon is a very talented painter himself. At first Kiall seemed, if not to like him, to admit he was good at his job. But when he began to take an interest in me—he stayed with us to take an inventory—Kiall changed.'

'So what does your mother think?' Ally turned to her. 'Surely her opinion is more important?'

'Mum's opinion important?' Sacha said in a derisive tone. 'Mum's opinions were so ruthlessly squashed, she doesn't know how to venture one any more. I could weep.'

'Don't tell me your brother is . . . intolerant with her?' Ally asked, almost hotly.

'Take it easy, sweetie.' Sacha threw her a quick look. 'Kiall is kindness itself.'

'Thank God for that! Quite a guy!'

'It's more a question of what do you do after a lifetime of being put down or ignored? Nobody seems to know why Father married again. You can be quite certain Mum didn't touch his heart.'

'Perhaps he wanted children?' Ally ventured, upset.

'There were any number of women milling about after Adele took off. Suitable women, that is, but he up and married someone very ordinary like Mum.'

'Perhaps he feared if she were too extraordinary history might repeat itself.'

'I suppose so, I've such high hopes you'll be able to help us, Ally. You're so beautiful and bright and clever. No one can put you down, and dear Karen sure tried. "You must hate being so tall,"' Sacha mimicked Karen's clear, patronising tones.

'I haven't grasped her exact position here,' Ally said with humour.

'She's staying for a few days. Invited herself. Never asks Mum directly. Mum would agree to anything if she thought it was what Kiall wanted.'

'I could have sworn he did.'

'Who knows with Kiall?' Sacha shook her curly blonde head. 'Providing heirs for Mowana might be Kiall's only reason for getting married. He's thirty-four, and there have been quite a few women in his life.'

'I'll bet!' Ally exclaimed feelingly, and then laughed. 'He's a stunning-looking man, and he's in terrific shape financially.'

'Karen's the pits!' Sacha burst out wrathfully. 'She even had the cheek to tick me off about Leon. As if it concerns her.'

'Maybe she was speaking as your soon-to-be sister-in-law,' Ally teased.

'When that happens,' said Sacha, 'I'll bolt.'

Ally took to Susan Lancaster immediately. The sweet face and the modest manner roused all her protective instincts. Some women were especially vulnerable, and a man of legendary harshness could only bring Susan emotional catastrophe. This, Ally believed, was what had happened. Despite Sacha's having called her mother 'ordinary', Ally didn't find her ordinary at all. Her looks were far from insignificant. In fact, with only a little attention she could be very pretty. Ally, the professional, knew she could transform her. All the basics were there. Susan had taken reasonably good care of her figure. She had good eyes, good hair, good skin. she had a shy grace, good humour and warmth. All that was missing was little pride in herself. No one could make the most of herself without confidence, and confidence was the missing ingredient. Ally, who had developed a self-discipline that was to last her all her life, longed to help. Sacha, who took the greatest pleasure making herself as dazzling as she possibly could, was somehow losing sight of her mother, the *woman*. Susan Lancaster was only in her early forties. Scarcely ready to be dusted off and put away. She had plenty of time to find the happiness that had eluded her. It was a characteristic of Ally to want to help even when no one thought to ask.

'I hope you're going to be very happy with us, Allegra,' Susan was now saying, showing Ally into a bedroom the size of a tennis court.

'Ally, please. It's Alison, really, after my mother. My modelling agency thought up Allegra. The very ultimate in sophistication.'

Susan laughed at the sparkling mockery of Ally's tones. 'You're very beautiful,' she said sincerely. 'I don't think I've ever seen your exact tawny colouring. It must be rare.'

'You haven't seen my mum.' Ally walked with her long, graceful glide to the wide veranda, looking out. 'This is heaven, isn't it?'

'*I* think so, but it can get very lonely.'

Ally stood and took deep breaths of the sweet, scented air. 'My first thought was that the homestead resembled a medieval fortress. It's the most astonishing thing, a silver stream completely surrounding it.'

Susan came to stand beside her. 'There are more than a hundred species of birds on the lagoon. It's a fauna sanctuary, actually. Black swans, pelicans, ducks, of course, jabirus and brolgas. You'll be able to see the brolgas perform their ballets.

The jabirus are our only storks. They make their large nests of sticks in the rain-forest.'

'So beautiful!' Ally watched the now late-afternoon sun slanting across the extensive lawns and lavish, long-established gardens. The rioting colours were fabulous, especially the towering displays of bougainvillaea in at least a dozen varieties—rose-pink, yellow, white, cerise, purple. They set the landscape ablaze. 'Thank you so much for having me.'

Susan smiled at the warm sincerity, the colour rushing into her cheeks. 'It's lovely to have you here, Ally. It gets very lonely when I'm on my own.'

'Why don't you travel around with Sacha from time to time?'

'Sacha doesn't want to be burdened with her mother,' Susan protested.

'You're kidding. The places I've taken *my* mother! The best thing about earning big money is that I can make things a lot easier for my parents. Dad will accept a little treat now and again, but my mother had developed a taste for a little travel. Only two weeks at a time, mind you. Dad and the farm come first, but we do enjoy ourselves.'

'Is your mother beautiful like you?' Susan smiled.

'Do you want to see a picture of her?' Ally walked back into the bedroom. 'I always carry one.'

'I'd love to.' Susan sank down on the huge, four-poster bed, deriving extraordinary comfort from the ease of Ally's manner.

Ally hunted up her handbag, took out her wallet and showed Susan the small, plastic-encased photograph she always carried.

'Oh, I can see the strong likeness,' Susan said.

Ally sat down companionably beside her. 'She's really something, my mother.'

'I can imagine, if she's like you.'

'Actually, she's not. Mum is a very sweet person. I'm bright and breezy. When I started growing, Mum thought I would never stop. I happen to be the only tall one in our family. Dad blamed it on the country, the climate. He thought it had to be all the food and the sunshine. My family emigrated from the UK when I was only two.'

'Good friends already?' Sacha, who had given orders for dinner, walked into the bedroom, taking in the companionable atmosphere.

'You've got a lovely mother,' Ally told her.

'I'm not complaining,' Sacha smiled.

No, but you *are* overlooking your mother's needs, Ally thought sadly. Susan wasn't happy, neither was she unhappy, but she was obviously unfulfilled.

Ally dressed for dinner in a body-hugging silk jersey, topaz in colour and very sensuous and soft. Her luxuriant mane, so beautiful cut, fell into thick, deep waves around her face, and she moved a little closer to the mirror to pull forward a stray curl. As a model she was able to do her hair in a dozen different ways, but she always thought long and loose was her best look. It complemented her oval, high-cheekboned face and balanced her height. A beautiful head of hair was a great asset, not only to the professional and Ally had worked out a care programme for every aspect of her appearance. By now she had it down to a fine art, a regimen for good health and good looks. Looking good affected one's state of mind, but Ally's underlying train of thought was the desire to do something for Susan. With the knowledge she had gained, she could transform Sacha's mother so that everyone would sit up and take notice. Susan could surely afford anything she wanted, but underneath the soft smile was a deep-seated depression. Susan had spent years of her life without a true identity, and that was the closest thing to oblivion. A woman was only beautiful to herself and to others when her spirit was free.

Susan had told her to treat the homestead like her own, so Ally left her room with the intention of exploring the major reception rooms, one of the rewards of being early.

The aborigines called the place the homestead was built on Mowana, which meant 'many waters,' and the Lancasters had prospered in their wild kingdom, carving out a great pastoral empire. The original core of the house, built entirely of cedar, included the central hallway, the great drawing-room with its six sets of french doors opening on to the verandas, the formal dining-room, the master bedroom and two others. The original kitchen wing, still preserved, had been built entirely separate, in case of fire. Wings had been added over the long span of the years so that the homestead was now massive. It was remarkable to consider that such a splendid and sophisticated construction had been built so soon after settlement, and against such daunting odds. No bark and slab huts for the Lancasters, but memories of the homeland. In the young Australia, a pastoral homestead was equivalent to a castle and certainly the great pioneering families had lived like lords.

The house looked splendid by night, the brilliant light from multiple chandeliers showing up the beautifully executed plastered ceilings and the richly carved cedar joinery. The paintings Sacha had spoken of were everywhere, overwhelming, really, and though the furniture and antiques everywhere displayed were magnificent, no attempt had been made at refurbishment for years. Curtains, upholstery, even lampshades needed replacing and, though still immensely distinguished, the house was like a beautiful woman whose radiance had been allowed to dim. There was no trace of an attempt at restoration, although Sacha had said her half-brother had become worried about the state of the art collection. Hence the entry of Leon Keppler into their lives. A man with so many demands on his time, and a huge station to run, surely could not be expected to take on the domestic arrangements as well? Susan and her daughter had obviously decided for one reason or another to leave well alone. It was the sort of house one had to approach with great confidence, but surely a firm of interior decorators could have been brought in and given *carte blanche*? Not that she would do that herself, Ally decided, she always had plenty of ideas of her own.

Ally was just crossing the wide, parqueted hallway when she heard a woman's voice uplifted in a kind of passion. Karen Fulbrook. Instantly Ally withdrew, slipping into the nearest room; what was now a sort of gun-room, where she huddled back against a wall. How embarrassing!

The voice came from perhaps the library, and one of the great double doors had to be open because Ally could clearly hear every word.

'I have an instinct about these things, Kiall,' Karen Fulbrook was saying.

'I know you're good at running people down,' he returned crisply.

'I wasn't aware of that.' The voice throbbed with great hurt.

'Come off it, Karen. I've been through all kinds of scenarios with you.'

'She's trouble, Kiall.'

Trouble? Ally gripped her throat.

'She's only just arrived.'

'I can promise you she'll encourage Sacha in some foolishness.'

'Susan seems to trust her,' Kiall Lancaster answered slowly, almost offhandedly.

'Susan's a fool.'

'Susan is my stepmother,' he reminded her tersely.

'I'm sorry, Kiall.'

'It would be nice if you'd remember she's also your hostess.'

'I said I'm sorry.' A short silence. 'I'm all on edge. How do you know she doesn't know this Leon Keppler?'

'I'm certain she doesn't.' The answer was toneless.

'These . . . *career women* know everyone. Mostly men.'

'Nose out of joint?' A deliberate taunt.

'Her looks don't impress me at all,' Karen told him. 'Honeypots don't have much distinction.'

'I wonder why she reminds me of a goddess,' he said brutally.

'Be serious, Kiall,' she begged him. 'We go back a long time. For ever. I know you're worried about Sacha.'

'Damn it, Karen, Sacha is *my* worry!' Anger leapt into the vibrant voice.

'We're good friends, aren't we? We really care about one another. Let me talk to this Allegra. I can put her straight.'

'You don't have to do that,' he warned her. 'Besides, from what I've seen of Miss Allen, she can more that hold her own.'

'Well, she had a huge advantage, being so tall,' Karen flared sarcastically.

'A little more of this, Karen, and I might have to ask you to leave.'

'You'd never!'

'On the contrary.'

'You're a cruel devil, aren't you?' she whispered. 'Just like your father.'

'An improved version, I assure you,' returned Kiall with hard mockery.

'You want to punish me.'

'Actually, I was trying to focus my attention on these reports.'

'Reports aren't likely to make you happy, or give you sons.'

'Don't go primitive on me, Karen,' he groaned.

'Why don't you make love to me any more?'

From embarrassment, Ally experienced a mad desire to escape. She moved quickly and very quietly, intending to back down the corridor, when a deep, bell-like gong sounded through the house, nearly startling her out of her wits.

Her hand flung up, the outstretched palm touching an ornament, a tiny little thing, no more than a silver trinket box, but it went crashing to the floor pretty much like a boulder in a quarry.

The silence was shattering.

Oh, God! Ally thought frantically, Karen Fulbrook, followed by Kiall Lancaster, still in his working-gear, appeared at the door.

'What on earth are you doing there?' Karen demanded, black eyes flashing lightning bolts.

'Listening, what else?' Ally tried for humour.

'Shocking manners—if you had any.'

Ally picked up the trinket box and restored it to the table. 'Please, it wasn't intentional.'

'How much did you hear?' Kiall Lancaster's gleaming eyes slid over her with malice.

'A lot of melodramatic dialogue. After that, I put my fingers in my ears. Listen, I'm sorry. I apologise. I came down early with the intention of exploring this wonderful house. Susan said I might.'

'Susan is not the judge of character she thinks she is,' Karen Fulbrook said severely.

'I've been told you're here often.'

'And what does that mean?'

'You want me to explain?' Ally said, laughing lightly. 'Forgive me, Mr Lancaster, I would never dream of invading your privacy. I slipped in here in case you were walking past the door. I had no wish to embarrass you. One gets locked into these moments, as I'm sure you know.'

'And obviously you want to keep your reputation going.'

She made a valiant effort not to blush. 'I have some good news, at any rate. I'm not here to pervert the course of justice. I'm here as Sacha's friend. I do *not* know Leon Keppler. I've never had the pleasure.'

'But you're on Sacha's side?' Karen accused, her finely cut mouth tightening.

'I intend to listen intently and try to give good advice.'

'If you have any to offer.'

'That's not very nice. I came to spend my time with Sacha and her mother. I'm a guest in this house. As you are. Being unpleasant is not my style.'

'You're a darling, Allegra,' Kiall Lancaster told her drily. 'Now, what about we dress for dinner? Life's getting to be one long, hard grind.'

'Friends, Miss Fulbrook?' Ally asked as the petite Karen swept by her.

'That's fine with me.' Karen tilted her dark head even further and rushed on.

'I really am sorry.' Ally turned back to Kiall Lancaster, apologising.

'Sure you're not being clever?'

'What, trying to catch the two of you alone?'

'I can promise you you won't do that.' He crossed the room to tower over her, and Ally felt compelled to fall back.

'Do you always inspire fanaticism in a woman?'

'Karen and I are old friends.' His startling eyes were roving all over her, bringing a warm flush to her body.

'Special friends?'

'Occasionally.' His mouth was a contradiction, firm, controlled, purely cut yet somehow sensual. He might be master of himself and every situation, but he was still a passionate man.

'I'm sorry I asked,' Ally found herself swallowing convulsively.

'Oh? You have some personal interest in me?'

'I'd like to give you a good going over, as in teach you a lesson. I think you're the sort of man who rides roughshod over a woman. You who rule the earth . . .'

'God, not another one on an ego trip?'

'Another one indeed. You don't know what the new woman is all about.'

'Tell me,' he invited acidly.

'I'd be delighted, but you'll be late for dinner.'

'Then tell me how you came by your prejudices. You don't know a damn thing about me.'

'I know you like to belittle women.'

'You?' He let his eyes rake her tall, willowy frame.

'At our first meeting you treated me like the chauvinistic *cochon* you are. You had no thought for my plight. You judged me out of hand. I was expected to endure your insults in utter submissiveness, then get shown the door.'

'So you're asking me to believe you weren't having an affair with Prentice?' Lamplight burnished his skin.

'Prentice? Not a chance. Do you have so little faith in women, you believe we all lie?'

'My dear Allegra,' said Kiall harshly, 'I've been taught to be very suspicous of women. Especially women like you. Would you say you're above seduction?' His eyes lowered to the curves of her breasts, causing sensation to glide all over her skin.

'I honestly can't. For instance, I wouldn't be above trying to seduce you.'

'So why don't we get started?' he challenged her, his voice tight and ruthless. 'No time like the present.'

'I'd say yes, only I don't want to upset the establishment!'

'How?' He tipped up her chin so firmly, she had no choice but to look up at him.

'I understand a model might be considered vulgar.'

'For what? You're way ahead of me.'

'A pity. The only man I'd work on would have to offer marriage.'

There was a subtle change in his eyes. 'You're asking me to marry you?'

'No way. You're so arrogant, you scare me.'

'Oh, I don't think you scare easily.' He touched a finger to the pulse in her throat.

'I won't allow this.' Under the mettle was desperation.

'Yes, you will.'

She had the absolute certainty that anything he wanted he got. A perfect thoroughbred, a beautiful painting, a woman. 'You'll get no co-operation.'

'You surprise me. I would have thought the awareness was mutual.' He slid his arm around her waist, welding her body so close to him that Ally had the searing sensation that the very core of her had melted. Hot colour stood out in patches on her beautiful, creamy skin.

'You have the most luscious mouth,' he said hypnotically. 'Open it for me.'

She managed a brittle smile. 'What an imperfect world we live in! Man the master, woman the slave.'

Desire, like some great jungle cat, padded dangerously between them. 'As a slave, you'd be a washout.' With his expert knowledge of women he had divined her response. He lowered his dark head and Ally shuddered. Actually shuddered, as though she was about to be devoured. Kiall used his sexual magnetism like a weapon.

Her head was whirling, and despite herself her heavy lashes fluttered down. The situation had got out of hand, and now she knew she couldn't deal with it.

The first touch of his mouth enslaved her senses. Sensation overwhelmed her in a sickening rush, she who thought she had her emotional life in order. The tip of his tongue played over the full, sensuous curves of her lips, but Kiall made no move to force entry to the moist interior. He was holding her in a very firm, controlling grip, so that for the first time in her life her natural spirit and self-assertiveness was vanquished by raw, male power.

His kiss blotted out every other kiss Ally received. It made her see things about herself she had never seen before. She had a capacity for passion that seemed suddenly terrifying. She was committing something vital, and she was committing it to him. Her lips parted like the petals of a flower, so that his powerful body momentarily tautened in reaction; then he was kissing her passionately, exploring her mouth to the limit of intimacy.

Her long, slender legs buckled under her, so that Kiall held her to him ruthlessly, fused at breast and thigh.

'Don't . . . ' she uttered. It was a plea for survival, pure and simple.

'Why don't you acknowledge a master?' He lifted his head, his extraordinary eyes glittering in a taut, sexually aroused face. The lines that ran from nostril to mouth were longer, deeper, suggesting tension.

'This is crazy. *You're* crazy!'

'Why not? *You've* always been.'

Instantly, the old, suppressed rage began to boil up in her. He carried his heritage in too tangible a form. The holy male, master of his destiny, but no master of *her*! She threw back her head so that her gleaming hair flew in an amber curtain.

'Who are you, anyway?' she demanded in a low, throbbing voice. 'You're not the only one around here with rights.'

'No, but it is my house,' he told her acidly. 'Please don't start on that feminist twaddle—I know you.'

'The hell you do!'

'Watch yourself, Allegra,' he warned her. 'There's a potential for violence there.'

'Let me go.' Her pearly teeth snapped together.

'No need for antagonism. *You* deal in seduction. *I* deal in action. You've been challenging me from the word go. Now I feel obliged to teach you a lesson.'

'Like rape?' she demanded furiously, superbly lithe from her workouts, but as helpless as a two-year-old against his strength.

'Has it been done before?'

'Why, you . . . *bastard*!' Ally half broke away from him in a paroxysm of rage. She was incandescent, beyond caution. Flashpoint! She threw back her arm, then brought up her hand, with its long, polished nails, and hit him as hard as she could across his insolent face. Her anger and excitement were unbounded.

'Stop that!' Kiall's formidable face shadowed, gathered power. He caught her wrist, his tone deadly quiet, but it shook her like an earthquake. 'I don't take that kind of treatment from anyone.' The imprint of her spread fingers had reddened his copper skin.

'Neither do I!' She stared up at him fierily, colour flaring beneath her beautiful skin.

'Why, look at you, you're trembling!' His narrowed eyes levelled over her, insolent, mesmerising.

'Rage might be part of it. Would you please let me go?'

'Certainly, but I think you like to be manhandled,' he taunted her.

Furious tears filled her eyes, and Ally turned away, blinking. 'I'd expect that from a man who lives to dominate.'

'I wasn't the one flexing my muscles,' he told her slender back.

'If you think I'm going to apologise, think again.'

Unexpectedly, he laughed. 'I'll tell you this. You pack a mean punch.'

'I can also shoot.' She spun about, looking as beautiful and wild as a lioness in the jungle.

'Really?' His amazing eyes lit up with laughter. 'Come to think of it, I can see you in the Annie Oakely role.'

'I'm just letting you know I can take care of myself.'

Their confrontation had generated so much heat, Ally had to lift the long, damp hair from her nape.

'You couldn't the first time I laid eyes on you,' he said with some satisfaction.

She shrugged her shoulders, throwing up her head and displaying her swan neck. 'In those days the things men got up to left me speechless. Now I'm clued up.'

'So!' His low laugh was sharp and derisive. 'Did Prentice sleep with you?'

'You'll never know for sure.' Her delicate nostrils flared.

'He said he did.'

'Wishful bloody thinking! But surely that was more than enough for you. The brotherhood and all that?'

'Oh God, gimme a drink,' he groaned with wry humour. 'I can't live with that, Ally.'

'No, you can't,' she agreed, her eyes startled. 'Even years ago I thought you were over-reacting. Come to that, I'm still at a loss.'

'Maybe I don't like to see silly young girls mauled by predatory men.' He picked up a crystal tumbler.

'Are there any others?'

'It makes it difficult when you women enjoy it.'

'I'll have you know I loathed Prentice.' She stalked toward him with her tawny litheness. 'So much for being virtuous!'

'At least you're now wearing clothes that fit!' His ironic gaze slid over her.

'I'll have you know I was very clever dressmaker,' she protested. 'Are you keeping all that whisky for yourself?'

'Forgive me.' He gave a sweeping bow. 'Say when.'

His lean, powerful body was imbued with a magnetic grace. 'Just a wee dram,' Ally answered. 'Usually when I drink I can't stop talking.'

'So when do you ever do that?'

'Women who talk up must be relatively new to you,' she

returned drily. 'Say, this is good!'

'Glenfiddich. I'd expect that from a girl whose mother hailed from the Highlands. Susan reminded me of it less than an hour ago. She was commenting on your splendid colouring. Very little happens around here I'm not told,' he added.

'I got that impression.'

'Have you met Leon Keppler?' he asked her, sitting back against a desk.

'Do you never take no for an answer?'

'Not right now. From you.'

Ally sighed and looked down into her glass. 'Have you ever thought opposition only makes Sacha more determined?'

'You think I should invite him here?' His eyes sparkled contemptuously.

'You want to know what's going on?'

'True.'

'I'm on Sacha's side.'

'So, my dear Allegra, am I,' he said his tone dry as dust.

'It's Alison, really. I should have told you, plain old Alison.'

'Why don't you use it? It's a name that could be coming back.'

'Allegra is the sort of name you use when you want to arrive. Anyway, I have not met Leon Keppler, so I can't decide if I don't like him. Are you so very sure, and one would have to be very, very sure, that his main interest in Sacha is her inheritance?'

'I wouldn't give him the time of day.'

'Why, because he's an art dealer? Shall we say, not exactly macho?'

'Don't be so damned silly,' said Kiall shortly. 'My objection to him is not because he's a bit odd, but because I have a gut feeling he's crooked.'

'Check him out,' Ally suggested.

'My dear girl, I've already had him investigated. He's a

a cleanskin.'

'Ever the cattle baron.' Ally put her glass aside. 'Then the bottom line is that *intuitively* you're against him?'

'We men do have it in some small way.' He thrust his hand through his hair, suggesting some inner disturbance. 'You're an outrageous girl, do you know that?'

'I'm a woman,' she told him, her golden eyes glowing with an inner fire.

'Better yet.' He laughed and went to walk past her. A curl had broken away from his widow's peak, lying on his forehead in rakish fashion. He was so tall and dynamic, Ally moved back automatically to give him plenty of room. 'By the way . . . '

'Yes?' Her eyes were huge with emotional assault.

'Fix your lipstick,' he told her. 'Someone might notice you're not wearing any.'

'Correct. Good old Karen, for sure.'

'You're bright, Ally,' he said drily! 'But not bright enough to catch me.'

'I wouldn't even try if I had any sense.' My God, what was she embroiled in?

He gave a mocking smile, as if he could see right through her. 'Your first night on Mowana.'

'So? My life hasn't changed.'

'Sheer bravado!'

It had but it would take her a long time to acknowledge it.

CHAPTER THREE

ALLY awoke next morning to golden, slanting sunlight. In place of the muted roar of traffic, a wonderful orchestration of birdsong from the tamarind trees. Sweet piercing cadences rose and fell, and she settled deeply into the grove of lace-trimmed pillows, feeling a sense of unreality.

Palest lemon voile curtained her bed, increasing the feeling of fantasy, and Ally stared up into the pitched canopy, admiring the golden *putti* that appeared to hold it in place. The splendours of yesteryear! The bedroom suite, though huge by her standards, was in keeping with the scale of the room. It had been chosen for a woman—*what* woman—because it was wondrously feminine, being carved and painted in ivory-pink. She thought it was French. There was a marvellous Récamier sofa as well between the pair of french doors. The walls were lined with nineteenth-century paintings, landscapes and flowers, and one of an adorable little white terrier with a blue ribbon around its neck on a rose-coloured cushion. The chintz that had been used on the chairs, the long bedstool and the curtains, though very faded, was wonderfully pretty—huge bouquets of cabbage-rose garlanded in green. There was a circular table with a rose-pink moiré skirt, two delicate chairs, and on the table several beautiful books on art and antiques, a collection of small boxes and a celadon vase filled with masses of a spectacular pink lily that grew in great drifts in the garden. It had to belong to the amaryllis family, but Ally had never seen the exact flower before. It was all so beautiful and enduring, and she responded to it strongly. Some people were extremely fortunate to have lived all their lives in a beautiful home. Such houses had a tremendous emotional pull. She could appreciate the great depth of feeling Kiall Lancaster had for his inheritance. He had told her himself, 'Mowana is my life.' And why not?

Overnight, the whole tenor of her life had changed. From emotional security, she was as quavery as a schoolgirl, shaken to the deepest depths of her being. She had seen herself, her high principles and her seemingly unshakable poise, only in terms of her relationships with a string of male admirers. She had been almost twenty-one before she had had her first real affair. His name had been Steven. He was a talented architect and musician, and they had fallen in love. At the time, she had thought it was the most important thing that had happened to her. Steven was very bright, very motivated. He knew what he wanted out of life. Ally had credited him with real intergrity, until she'd learned that he had been seeing an old girlfriend as well. She had ended it that day, though he had protested over and over that the other girl meant 'less than nothing' to him. He was deeply in love with *her*. What was more, he really believed that. It was obviously an inherent disorder of the male. Infidelity. Strangely enough, she had not suffered, and she saw now that it was because she had never really been in love. Since then, her experience had been far from extensive, but she knew what it was to be made love to by an attractive and sophisicated man. She had even confided to a friend that she had the dismal feeling that real passion would escape her, like most people; now she had come in for a tremendous jolt. Her confrontation with Kiall Lancaster had struck at the very centre of her being. Perhaps it was profoundly biological but, whatever it was, it was extremely powerful.

Ally lay back on her pillows, reflecting on the scene at dinner last night. She wasn't the only one with a few model's tricks. Sacha needed male company other than a brother to move her to special attention, but Karen Fulbrook knew what making the most of herself was all about. So slim and petite, she had developed a personal style, very neat and streamlined, defining her assets. Her glossy hair hugged her well-shaped head, her dark eyes were made up to look huge and her polished, sun-tanned skin looked its best against a seductive little number shaped as simply as a *maillot* in matt white. A light, very expensive fragrance hung around her, and Ally, ever fair, gave her an all-over ten for grooming and presentation. There was a big difference in her rating for warmth and charm, although she did have a decided, dangerous wit. A blind woman would have noticed she was madly in love with Kiall Lancaster. In fact, it was so noticeable, it was painful. Surely women strayed into the area of greatest vulnerabilty when they so openly exposed their hearts? Ally, who liked a to keep a man guessing as much as humanly possible, actually pitied her. Did women like Karen form their deepest attachments with men who could only make them suffer? At some point in their lives they must have been lovers, perhaps they were now, but it seemed to Ally that Kiall Lancaster had made it perfectly clear he wasn't having any. Marriage, that was. Tough as he was now, she knew he could still remember the terror of an abandoned six-year-old. Perhaps he was afraid to fall in love. It happened like that. Loving, for him, had meant a terrible separation and pain. To love was to lose. He had been brought up by an embittered father to believe certain women were destructive, women clearly recognised as outstandingly female. His mother had proved it, breaking her sacred vows and deserting her small son.

For her own part, Ally wanted her own involvement to stop there. She knew now that emotions out of control could be terrifying. Kiall Lancaster was a powerful and disturbing man. Moreover, he was extremely complex. Falling madly in love with him wouldn't alter anything, and she wasn't look for emotional trauma. She was a successful woman in her own right. Even as a top-flight model she knew she had to face a short working life, but Zoe had already spoken about her taking over the agency. Zoe was coming to the stage when she wanted to retire, and she looked on Ally as a daughter. The two women were very close, and Zoe had every confidence in Ally's ability to take her place. It looked like a safe, secure job for life. Love affairs were not, and, what was more killing, the institution of marriage was not what it once had been, either. Ally had been bridesmaid to a fellow model who had been crying buckets within a month. Six months later it had been over, and Ally had spent the following year trying to help her friend out of an abysmal depression. Falling in love was highly risky. Falling in love with Kiall Lancaster amounted to crisis.

Nevertheless, Ally lay in bed remembering the touch of his mouth on her own. The exercise caused such an uprush in her blood, she jumped out of bed as if under threat. The truth of it was that Ally, the reasoned feminist, was desperately scared. Allowing him to kiss her had been a suicidal gesture. She should be very, very grateful it had stopped there. Imagine allowing him full possession of her body! Clearly when she was so reactive it could only be ecstasy, but what would she do afterwards, throw herself in front of a bus? Playing with fire made no sense at all.

Ally drew on her matching satin *peignoir* and walked out on to the veranda. Magnificent golden canes in huge terracotta pots blocked the bedrooms from one another, and down the length of the long, deep veranda rattan chairs and tables had been set at intervals. It was a magnificent private kingdom, but Ally could quite see the management of the homestead could become a burden. Much as she liked Susan, she could see Susan wasn't up to it. Great possessions could amount to a great burden. The people who accepted such burdens willingly were special. In a way, looking after a mansion had to be an obsession. Although Mowana wasn't the sort of stately house Charles Lancaster had been born in, or indeed anything like it, for recent times and in a new land it was very impressive indeed. In the right hands it could be brought to appropriate life. There was no question, it needed redecorating and lightening in a way that fitted into the mood of comtemporary life. Ally, who was really very domesticated, considered the homestead needed a new cook as well. Even with the best of everything to hand, dinner last night had been surprisingly dull and ordinary. 'Good plain food,' her father would have called it, but Ally would have sent the housekeeper, a woman not unlike Mrs Danvers, on a cookery course, or failing that, packing. Susan was plainly in awe of her, which meant Susan's cooking had to be even worse, and the master of the house, who had to be hungry after a long, hard day's work, had plunged into his meal without enthusiasm. Probably he had been reared on such fare, and boarding-school and university canteens wouldn't have provided him with much relief. It was extraordinary, really. Though considered the rich and privileged, there was something very wrong at Mowana. The mistress didn't fit, and the master found every excuse not to change her.

Ally's mind was so occupied with her thoughts, she failed to notice Kiall Lancaster cross a path at the side of the house and walk up and along the veranda towards her.

'Good morning, dear Alison.'

Ally turned swiftly, blinking into the sun. A beam of light played over her tawny-gold hair and the slender length of her body. His crystal eyes were bold.

'Where did *you* come from?' Ally inched her *peignoir* further on to her shoulders. Her nightgown was cut to a deep V, revealing the creamy slopes of her breasts.

'The stables,' he told her, not taking his eyes off her. 'I've been up since dawn.'

'You're kidding!'

'No exaggeration at all. I've been up for hours.'

'You know what they say, too much work makes Jack a dull boy.'

'Do *you* find me dull?' he queried sardonically.

'I think you're making progress.'

'So . . . ' he leaned back against the balustrade. 'Did you sleep well?'

'Like a top. I've never slept in such a splendid room.'

'My mother's.'

'Really?' Ally gave a convulsive swallow.

'It's about time we made use of it.'

'I thought it had a little hidden haunting.'

'I know what you mean. Everything about the house is haunted.'

'Oh, but I *love* it,' she said, as though he had reproached her. 'It has tremendous atmosphere.'

'It's run down.'

'*Never!*' Ally threw her expressive hands in the air. 'It's a splendid house, as you very well know.'

'Are you going to tell me it couldn't do with some redecorating?' he challenged her.

'Well . . . ' She shrugged a sloping shoulder. 'People who love their homes are more or less always refurbishing.'

'Little has been touched since my mother left.' A very glittery look, came upon him, high-mettled and edgy.

'Why not?'

'I suppose no one had the heart to try. My father never really accepted she wouldn't come back to him. You can imagine what that did to Susan. It robbed her of all confidence. All the years of her marriage were very damaging.'

'So why did she marry your father?' Ally asked quietly.

'She thought she could get him to love her. After all, she

loved *him.*'

Ally gave a deep sigh. 'I don't know what it is about women that makes us take so much punishment.'

'She survived it.'

'There's a price.'

'One has to learn early to depend on oneself.'

'I suppose so!' Ally walked to the edge of the balustrade, and looked out. 'I take it money's no object?'

'For what?'

'Redecorating, what else?' She turned her head to look at him.

'I'm certain if I told you I was a multi-millionaire it would be no surprise.'

'Someone did give me that valuable piece of information, Mr Lancaster,' she said airily. 'Have you ever said to Susan, "Get the decorators in"?'

'I'm looking for a woman who can do it herself.'

'You can scarcely put Karen above your stepmother,' said Ally dubiously.

'Karen's taste is not mine,' he retorted bluntly. 'The Lancasters have always decorated with an English accent, if you know what I mean. I think if Karen had her way she'd throw all the early-nineteenth-century furniture out—the paintings, the rugs, the objects, even the curtains and wallpapers. The Fulbrook homestead is very contemporary. I like it. It's interesting. It make a very contemporary statement, but it's not for me. I identify too closely with my forebears. This building, this homestead, is me.'

'And I understand completely.' Ally's eyes flashed with an answering brilliance. 'All the homestead needs is a little lightening. It could be achieved very easily. So much has been acquired over the years, things could be stored and rotated. New curtains and covers would make an enormous difference. There are so many glorious fabrics, all the wonderful early patterns recreated. I should think it would be tremendously exciting doing the house up. All the leading interior decorators would fall over backwards to get the commission.'

'It need professionals?' He gave her a straight, serious look.

'I think so. It's a very big house, and important in terms of our heritage. Good professionals work with the client.'

'Not me, I simply don't have the time.'

'Susan, Sacha?' she suggested.

'Sacha has no interest whatsoever,' he told her flatly. 'And Susan would want my approval all the time. I have to work. Depressing, I know.'

'Why don't you at least speak to her about it? Obviously it's on your mind.'

'Sure.' Unconsciously, Kiall's expression was full of a deep scepticism.

'Why don't I? As you're so busy.'

'You think you can turn Susan around?'

'That's awful!'

'You know perfectly well what I mean.'

Ally wasn't about to criticise her hostess. 'I'm a mentor in my own fashion,' she said carefully. 'I've been known to help people. I'm very interested in improving the quality of life for other women.'

He sat back, eyes shimmering with mockery. 'Sacha thinks you're perfect. Beautiful, glamorous, successful, good-humoured, a born achiever.'

'Why not?' she burst out. 'I firmly believe a woman can do anything she wants to.'

'I believe you.'

'Do you?'

'You looked surprised.'

'I was certain you were one of those lords of creation, all high mettle and hard, glittery edges.'

'How interesting! I can't say you're terribly wrong.' His

glance swept over her face and hair. 'Whatever happened to that mop of wild hair you used to have?'

'I got myself a good hairdresser.' She gave an exasperated sigh and pitched a hand into a deep, springing wave.

'I can still see you now.'

'I must have made an enormous impression,' she said airily.

'You were just so beautiful.'

Her delicate eyebrows rose. 'Are you telling me times are changing?'

'You're still beautiful, Ally,' he said drily. 'I guess you always will be. The bones are there.'

'Dear heaven! I have a few years left. I'm only twenty-four.'

'And you're in a cruel business. Surely thirty would be considered over the hill?'

'I have thought of doing other things with my life.'

'Like getting married?'

She looked at him steadily. 'I'd like to get married, yes. I adore children. Look, do you mind if I pop in and get dressed?'

'Am I disturbing you?' Kiall cocked his handsome head to one side.

'I don't think you've blinked once.'

'You can't object to that, Ally. In fact, you must be used to it.' His silver eyes danced with light.

Ally folded her satin *peignoir* closer around her body, a modest gesture that completely defeated its purpose. 'Most of the heavy staring passes me by.'

He nodded absently. 'That nightgown must have cost a lot.'

'Like it?' Ally murmured, and twirled about. She wasn't a top model for nothing.

'It's lovely. I'm almost in a trance. Tell me, have you a special friend now?'

'Why, thirty or forty,' she said flippantly.

'I often wondered what a beautiful young girl saw in

Prentice.'

Ally made a sound of total exasperation, and looked past him at the towering palms of the garden. 'There's no hope for you,' she said shortly.

'And what does that mean?' He stood up and walked towards her.

'You have to trust people, Kiall.'

'My dear girl, I trust lots of people.' He was close enough to enfold her in his arms, and Ally moved back restlessly.

'It's just you don't like women?'

'I like them,' he told her slowly. 'It's just I don't rate them as highly as men.'

'That's an idea that was dumped on you.'

He held up a palm, much as he would to a prancing horse. 'Whoa, Amber. I didn't bring you here to psychoanalyse me.'

'But I've already figured you out. At length.' She stared up into his electric eyes, unconsciously revelling in having him tower over her.

'Can you stop talking for a few minutes?' he asked drily.

'Sure I can.'

'There's no possibility you'll interrupt?'

'No.' She shut her delicious mouth firmly.

'How about your first riding lesson?'

She flung her head up, delighted. 'Great!'

'You're not scared?'

'Of course not. You're a nice man.'

He looked down his straight nose at her, unamused by her impudence. 'Be down at the stables in fifteen minutes.'

'Sure, boss.' She sketched a silly salute in defiance of his coolness.

He continued to look down at her for a brief, tingling moment, then he walked away abruptly. A moment later, Ally heard him laugh out loud on the path.

Men were like horses, she mused dreamily. All they needed

was breaking in.

The days went so swiftly, there simply weren't enough hours to fit everything in, nor for Ally to understand what was happening to her. She had her riding lesson every morning, and was progressing fast, due to the combination of a first-class teacher—he confounded her by being extremely patient—and her own natural athletic ability. In fact, Ally could often be found at the stables complex, admiring the outstanding beauty of the Arabs for Mowana had long distinguished itself as an Arabian stud-farm. Being blessed with an exceptionally kind temperament, Kiall had selected an old favourite, the pure-bred Yasmin, to carry her through her lessons. The breed was marked by essential characteristics: the dished profile, small, wedge-shaped head and wide forehead, the tapering muzzle and the large, brilliant eyes placed relatively low in the head. What Ally found most noticeable, apart from sweetness of expression and extreme grace of movement, was the way they carried their luxuriant tails as high as a banner the instant they went into action. Her own Yasmin, and she had begun to call her 'my girl', had a coat as silky and fine as could be imagined. Yasmin was, moreover, a bright chestnut, reinforcing Ally's own colouring and creating a special bond. The Arabian had always been considered the oldest and purest of breeds, and Ally didn't wonder they had always been associated with romance and legend.

'Great charisma surrounds the Arabs,' Kiall told her, pleased by her admiration and interest. In fact, he spent a good deal of his valuable time showing her around the stables and spinning a hundred and one tales about the breed, through the realms of fantasy to the fantastic price an American stud-farm, one of the largest in the world, had paid for their top stallion, Mowana Magic.

From there, Ally went to Mowana's extensive library, sitting up late in bed, reading all she could on Arabs. The more she read, the more fascinated she became. No one could help loving such beautiful animals as horses, but some special aura of romance clung to the classic Arab.

'If you ride, ride an Arab.'

That was the first thing Kiall said to her as he prepared her for her first lesson, and certainly Yasmin was a joy to learn on.

By the end of the first week Ally had been readily accepted into station life by all except Karen, who stayed and stayed, and perhaps Mrs Danvers, or Mrs Tanner as she was more properly known.

Ally, so interested in nutrition, felt there was absolutely no need for the menus to be so rigid—there was an unvaried one for every day of the week—or so unimaginative. It was scarcely her business, but she felt something had to be done. If the truth be told, she didn't like to see the master of the house, who worked dawn to dusk, eat out of habit and not enjoyment. He deserved better. They all deserved better. Ally had to say it for herself, she was a confirmed do-gooder. Sometimes it worked, sometimes it didn't. She thought she had to be an earth-mother.

Susan obviously felt comfortable with her, and it was a mutual thing; in fact, Ally got on better with Susan than Sacha appeared to. Because of this friendliness, Ally broached the subject one late afternoon. Mrs Tanner, looking very put-upon, had just served cold drinks, and Ally looked after her solid figure thoughtfully.

'She's not a fun person, is she?'

'A dragon,' Sacha seconded, 'and that's the truth.'

'She works terribly hard,' Susan said, trying to excuse the housekeeper's less than gracious attitude.

'I thought she was downright snarly right now. Not at all the image of the old family retainer.'

'She isn't.' Sacha sipped at her drink. 'An old family

retainer, that is. Most of them left with Kiall's mother. Mrs Tanner has only been with us five years. She replaced Rosa, a real dolly.'

'Doesn't she like too much direction in the kitchen?' Ally asked casually.

'Ally dear,' Susan said in a low voice, 'I don't interfere at all. I really don't want to go through a scene.'

Ally stared at Sacha, who pulled a face. 'You mean you can't walk into your own kitchen at any time?'

'Absolutely.' Sacha nodded her blonde head. 'As if I'd want to!'

'But Mrs Tanner could loosen up a little, don't you think? She tends to be too rigid.'

'Do you mean she's a rotten cook?' Sacha, who was always on a diet, wasn't terribly unhappy.

'Well, she's working with the finest ingredients. Sometimes it's a question of a little direction. There are so many books available. I'm sure anyone who was really interested could become an excellent cook. I know if I cooked for a living I'd have an immense repertoire. What's the use of doing anything if you're not going to do it well?'

'That's you, sweetie,' Sacha said. 'Some of us are plain lazy.'

'It's a pity, though.

'Something on your mind?' Sacha asked equably.

'We could approach her.'

'You'll have to, dear.' Susan looked almost fearful.

'Hey, you're the boss around here.' Ally touched her hand.

'Me?' Susan gave a funny little laugh and lay back in her wicker chair.

'Indeed. Mistress of Mowana. Mistress of an historic homestead,' Ally confirmed gaily.

'I'm not the mistress here, Ally.' The words seemed to burst from Susan's throat. 'I'm still the very ordinary girl Austin married after his beautiful wife left him. *She* was the mistress of Mowana. Everyone doted on her. Twenty years we shared, and I don't think I had my husband's full attention once.'

'Oh, come off it, Mum!' Sacha pleaded, embarrassed. The colour even rose to the fair line of her hair.

But Ally was more concerned with Susan. 'I'm certain he cared for you,' she murmured, looking deep into Susan's blue eyes. 'From every account he was a difficult man. Obviously he couldn't express it. People do have major hang-ups.'

'Do you know he used to call out her name in his sleep? Not occasionally, over the years, but continually.'

'Why do you talk about this, Mum?' Sacha demanded. 'It makes me desperate.'

'It's therapy, Sacha,' Ally said.

'None the less, it's embarrassing.'

'Not for me.' Ally reached over and patted Sacha's hand. 'We're friends, aren't we? All friends here. We all need relief. Telling someone. Didn't you tell me all about your troubles?'

'Of course, but nothing so terrible as Mum's story. I couldn't bear to live with a man who didn't love me.'

'When you think about it, do all that many people love together? There's always one who kisses and one who turns the cheek. It would be awful actually to leave someone you loved. Men seem to get terribly frightened of admitting love, and they seem to get more reticent over the years. I know my father would be bereft if, God forbid, anything happened to my mother, but I've never heard him say to her, "I love you." Maybe he says it when they're alone. I doubt it, but my mother knows perfectly well of their powerful attachment.'

'You're trying to be kind, Ally,' Susan said. 'I've never set any value on myself, so I could hardly expect anyone else to.'

'So, even if it's true, and I value your friendship, why shouldn't that change? Aren't we supposed to grow to the end of our days? Correction, I hope I don't grow to the end of my days.'

'Who wouldn't be tall if they could look like you?' Sacha sighed. 'Listen, why don't we keep these in-depth discussions to another time? I thought we were talking about cooking?'

'With your permission, Susan,' Ally said earnestly, 'I'd like to have a little chat with our Mrs Tanner.'

'I wish you luck!' Sacha waved her glass.

'Why don't you come with me? You're the daughter of the house.'

'I'm like Mum. I have an inability to cope.'

'Susan, may I?' Ally asked. 'I'll be as diplomatic as I know how.'

'Falling that, just give her the chop.'

'You don't mind do you, Ally?' Susan asked, as diffident as a schoolgirl.

'Of course I don't mind. I'll bet you're paying Mrs Tanner a good salary.'

'Plus she eats like a horse and drinks the brandy,' added Sacha.

'Then a few words are in order. Employees anywhere must expect a few directions.'

'Go to it then, girl,' Sacha said brightly. 'I suspected Leon wanted to say something when he was here.'

Ally waited until mid-morning of the next day, when things were quiet. Sacha was still at the pool pavilion, a magnificent area shaded by hundreds of palm trees, Susan was writing letters, and Karen, splendid horsewoman that she was, was accompanying Kiall on his morning rounds.

Mrs Tanner reigned in her domain, no ordinary kitchen this, but one Prue Leith would have lusted after. Ten qualified chefs could have worked happily at peak periods, such was its size and equipment. All the more reason for such a splendid culinary environment to be put to better use. After all, did a six-year-old learn to play the piano on a Steinway concert grand? Ally felt slightly hampered by the fact that she was a visitor, but Susan had quite happily delegated responsibility.

Mrs Tanner at that moment was standing at the kitchen sink, chewing something. She was a tallish, chunky woman with bright, sharp eyes and a formidable jaw.

'Ah, good morning, Mrs Tanner,' Ally said brightly, knowing full well she had been regarded with suspicion since the day she had arrived.

'Can I help you, miss?' Mrs Tanner turned, frowning, wiping her hands on her apron and blocking Ally's continuing progress. Her expression strongly exuded the message Ally had absolutely no business in the kitchen.

Ally kept the pleasant smile on her face. 'Yes, you can, Mrs Tanner. Mrs Lancaster has asked me to discuss menus with you.'

'Menus?' The formidable jaw dropped open, and snapping black eyes stared back at Ally as if she had gone mad.

'Of course,' Ally said. 'We thought we might try a few different things.'

'We?' Mrs Tanner now held herself stiffly erect.

'You, actually,' Ally said pleasantly. 'Why don't we sit down and have a cup of coffee?'

'I'm not hired to sit about, young lady,' Mrs Tanner said sternly, moving directly to confrontation, and she had a very booming voice.

'No,' Ally agreed reasonably, 'but you are hired as cook and housekeeper to the household. We feel—Mrs Lancaster feels you must be allowed to expand your skills to the limit. After all, creative people can't do their best work without encouragement.'

Mrs Tanner's red flush faded and astonishment set in. 'Do I understand you properly?'

'Please sit down, Mrs Tanner,' Ally said. 'We can discuss this more comfortably.' She indicated a chair with one beautiful, long hand.

'And who are you, may I ask?'

'I am, as you are aware, a family friend.' Ally returned levelly. 'I am speaking to you with Mrs Lancaster's full knowledge and approval.'

'I'll be here,' Mrs Tanner boomed formidably, 'if Mrs Lancaster wishes to speak to me herself.'

'Naturally, she'll be calling in later,' Ally said smoothly. 'But she's so busy this morning, I've been given this assignment. Sit down, Mrs Tanner.'

Mrs Tanner's normal wits weren't quite about her, for she obeyed, plonking herself stolidly on to a kitchen chair.

'You impress me as a very capable woman, Mrs Tanner,' Ally said earnestly. 'I'm sure you have a great knowledge of cooking and your kitchen is superb. May I compliment you on the way you keep it?'

Mrs Tanner was clearly startled. Resentment faded and she peered at Ally as though she couldn't begin to fathom what she was all about. 'Thank you,' she managed finally, 'I do my best. Now, what is all this about menus? Isn't Mr Lancaster happy with my services?'

'Oh, I'm sure he is,' Ally promised swiftly; after all, the woman was efficient in her own way. 'But Mr Lancaster is far too busy a man to have to concern himself with the domestic arrangements of the homestead.'

'Agreed. Mr Lancaster is a hero!' Mrs Tanner declared devoutly. 'The way he took me on after my husband ran off . . .'

'Oh, I'm so sorry,' Ally said, herself surprised by this revelation.

'He was supposed to be on leave of absence, but he never came back.'

'Work on the station, he did?'

'Leading hand. I used to cook for all the men.'

'Then Mr Lancaster must be very appreciative of you,' Ally

murmured. She could quite see Mrs Tanner turning out moutains of excellent scones and dampers and the like.

'Aye, he was. The men miss me, I'm told. Everyone surpported me when Ted left.'

'This was about five years ago?'

Mrs Tanner nodded. 'Mr Lancaster sent someone after him but, do you know, I refused to have him back?'

'You're a strong-minded woman, Mrs Tanner.'

'That I am.' Mrs Tanner sounded genuinely gratified.

'Do you get plenty of time off, a break away from the station?'

'No place else to go.'

'No family?' By this time, Ally was feeling quite sorry for Mrs Tanner.

'A daughter in New Zealand.'

'Do you visit her?' Ally asked, smiling.

'I'm terrified of planes.'

'Now that won't do,' Ally said. 'You must long to see her.'

'I do.' Under Ally's eyes, the formidable face softened into longing. 'Just had another baby, you know. Four now.'

Once started, Mrs Tanner waxed on about her grand-children for a good ten minutes.

'You could try short flights at a time,' Ally suggested in the first break. 'Have you actually been in an aeroplane?'

'Never.' Mrs Tanner's heavy frame shuddered. 'Mr Kiall's father, Mr Austin, was killed in a plane crash. I expect you know that.'

'Yes.' Ally bent her glowing head. 'But I understand he took a terrible risk. Men do take risks, don't they? They don't show the same caution as we women. I work as a fashion model for a living, and I've flown thousands and thousands of miles.'

'You can't like it?' asked Mrs Tanner sceptically.

'I love it,' Ally told her. 'But then I'm a bit of a fatalist. I believe when your time's up, it's up, no matter where or when.

I have the feeling it's all mapped out.'

'Maybe.' Mrs Tanner inclined her grey head. 'It's not so much I'm frightened, it's just I'd want to put my head through the window.'

Ally didn't laugh. 'I promise you, you wouldn't feel like that at all. There's plenty of air in the cabin. You can't let a little hang-up prevent you from seeing your daughter and grandchildren. Why don't you ask Mr Lancaster to take you up in the Beech Baron?'

Mrs Tanner's eyes bulged at the very idea. 'I'd never suggest such a thing!'

'Why not?'

'It wouldn't be me to forget my place.'

'If you don't ask him, I will,' Ally said supportively. 'I'm sure when he knows you're desperate to get to New Zealand he would take the fear out of flying for you. He's a marvellous pilot.'

Mrs Tanner was becoming more human by the minute. 'You think he would even consider it?' She stared into Ally's eyes.'

'My goodness, Mrs Tanner,' Ally said, 'weren't you the one to call him a hero?'

'I couldn't ask him.' Mrs Tanner shook her head regretfully.

'You don't have to. I'll just mention it in passing.'

'Would you?' For a big woman, Mrs Tanner jumped up in a very sprightly fashion. 'Why don't I make that cup of coffee?'

'Good idea.'

CHAPTER FOUR

NEVER one to lost time, Ally decided to approach Kiall that evening. She waited until the pre-dinner drink period and then went in search of him. Under his daunting exterior, and he exuded a male toughness, she felt there lurked a heart of gold. Hadn't he been 'kindness itself' to Susan when many another stepson, given total power, would have found some excuse to have her leave Mowana? He was vitally interested in Sacha's welfare, and every last employee on the station worshipped the ground he trod upon. She had an excellent chance to gain his ear. In fact, the element of chance had played a big part in her dealings with Mrs Tanner. Talking about her grandchildren had unlocked all the woman's warmth. It had even made it possible for them to discuss various dishes in perfect harmony. It turned out Mrs Tanner wasn't averse to a little experimentation, only waiting for the right sort of prodding. They had pored over beautiful big cookbooks, some of which contained step-by-step guides to foolproof results. And Mrs Tanner was no fool. She was an unhappy soul, with her own needs and fears. Communication was always the first step, or so Ally thought.

As soon as she stepped into the central hallway with its lovely *parquet de Versailles,* she was greeted by a familiar voice. 'Ah, there you are, Miss Allen! Would you mind coming this way?'

'And if I decide not to?' Ally was extremely irritated by Karen Fulbrook's cold, high-handed manner.

'Kiall wants to see you.'

'Fine. 'I'll see *him* any time,' Ally mocked.

63

'And what do you mean by that?' Karen challenged, arrested in mid-flight. With her ebony hair and eyes, and her golden-tanned skin, dressed in shimmering chartreuse, she looked very vivid and somewhat exotic.

'Who the heck are you, biting my head off?' Instinctively Ally reacted.

'Don't look for niceness from me,' Karen muttered urgently. 'I know what you're about.'

Ally straightened her spine and pulled back her shoulders. She looked down her perfect nose at the older girl's hostile face. 'Please tell me.'

'You'd gobble up Kiall if you could. I know your type. Man-eaters.'

'I've learned to live with it.'

'Then you admit it?' Karen's Egyptian eyes flashed.

'I think it has something to do with my looks. Actually, the epithet is quite unwarranted. I'm a quiet, good-living girl.'

'I can promise you, if you get in my way, you'll be sorry,' Karen warned.

'It's a good thing you're short. That's a blessing.'

'Don't fool with me.' Aggression thinned Karen's red mouth, so for a moment she looked quite ominous. 'Plenty have tried.'

'Did any finish in the morgue?' Ally laughed.

'You do like to be smart, don't you? Don't bat those absurd lashes at Kiall. He's for me!'

'Really?' Ally raised a delicate brow. 'If he is, he's not happy about it. Now, if you'll excuse me, I'll make my courtesy call.'

'And I'm coming with you.'

'Frightened I'm going to steal him from right under your nose?'

'This might be one courtesy call you won't like,' Karen sneered.

As they approached Kiall's study, she rushed ahead so that

she could precede Ally into the room. 'What goes on here?' Ally enquired. 'I can guarantee it's not a party.'

Karen swept across the glowing Persian rug and aligned herself beside Kiall, who was seated at his massive mahogany desk. The portrait of the first Charles Lancaster with a light on it, was directly behind him, above the mantelpiece. It had been painted by an acknowleged master, and the impression of power almost bounded out of the canvas.

'Karen tell me you've been upsetting Mrs Tanner,' Kiall said almost mildly, setting down some papers.

'It's not that way at all.' She met his eyes.

'What way exactly is it?' he asked smoothly.

'Has Mrs Tanner complained?' Ally asked.

'She complained to me,' Karen cried stormily.

'About what? Is it all right to sit down in court?' Ally moved back a few paces and sat in a burgundy leather chair. She crossed her long, slender legs, narrow feet encased in beautiful Italian shoes, and arched her ankles. Her dress was deep yellow silk, lending a glow to hair, skin and eyes.

Karen's small bosom heaved. 'It's fine for one of us to talk to Mrs Tanner, but not you. After all, you're a guest here.'

'You have a share in this house?' Ally feigned astonishment.

Karen ignored her. 'I really don't think you have a right to upset this household.'

'But it was fun!'

'Ask her to be serious, Kiall, please,' Karen urged, her small hand on his shoulder.

'Did you speak to Mrs Tanner about her cooking?' Kiall paid no attention to Karen, but looked at Ally directly.

'Yes, I did, after I'd spoken to Susan first. I can't accept Mrs Tanner was outraged. It seemed to me we got on perfectly well.'

'Yet you did suggest she try new recipes?'

'I did. I got a kick out of it.'

'You haven't been happy with what's been offered?'

'Don't worry about me,' Ally said. 'It's you I was concerned about.'

'Oh, how?' His winged black eyebrow shot up, a mannerism.

'I know the way to a man's heart is through his stomach.'

'Are you going to listen to this, Kiall?' Karen implored, almost wringing her hands. 'I can only take so much.'

'What would you like to do?' Ally asked her. 'Run me off the property? Don't answer that. I'm certain Miss Fulbrook is exaggerating,' she said to Kiall.

'Why don't we get Mrs Tanner in here?' He got up from his chair, his every movement as sleek and graceful as a big cat's.

'Why bother her now, Kiall?' Karen protested, suddenly backing down. 'She'll be busy with dinner.'

'I certainly hope so,' Ally said blithely. 'I'm predicting a few changes.'

'You take a lot upon yourself.' Kiall leaned back against his desk, staring at Ally's bright, burnished beauty.

'Never without good reason.' She didn't flinch from meeting those crystal eyes. 'Can you honestly tell me you've been enjoying your meals?'

'Maybe I have too much on my mind.'

'I, for one, think she has an appalling cheek,' Karen cried wrathfully.

'Probably you ate before you came.'

'You keep seeing yourself as a comedienne, don't you?' Karen said bitterly.

'I think it's high time you loosened up,' Ally suggested with perfect truth.

'I'm going to speak to Susan,' Karen said. 'I expect you're lying and took this whole thing on yourself.'

'Lying?' Ally threw up her chin. 'Why, my dear Miss Fulbrook, I'm simply not capable of it.'

Karen was actually quivering with anger and a queer excitement. 'Just you wait!' She all but flew out of the room, her full skirt whipping around her legs.

Ally turned her head and looked after her. 'Have you ever thought your girlfriend needs professional help?'

'Maybe you're not good for her.'

'Maybe you're not, either.'

'More than anything else, I need to be told my business by a woman.'

'Notwithstanding your attitude, Mr Lancaster, my concern is genuine. That girl's unstable.'

'Piqued as well.' His handsome mouth quirked. 'I expect she's been itching to give Mrs Tanner, a good talking to.'

'Speaking of Mrs Tanner,' Ally sprang up and walked towards him, 'she has a daughter in New Zealand. Did you know that?'

'Look, any time you want a job, I'll be happy to hire you. I don't have much time to talk to Mrs Tanner these days.'

'I appreciate that, Mr Lancaster,' she said sweetly, allowing her eyes the luxury of roaming over his striking face. It was much too strong and positive to be merely handsome. He had very high, definite cheekbones and the cheeks were hollowed. Little lines fanned out from his brilliant eyes, from crinkling them in the radiant sunlight. His darkly tanned skin was very fine-grained.

'Yes?' His expression mocked her.

'Sorry, what was I saying? Your presence is intoxicating.'

'Then what should we do about it?'

'Absolutely nothing,' she sighed. Loving a man like that could bring a lot of pain. 'I'm a woman who likes to keep her life in order.'

He put his hands to her narrow waist and drew her towards him. 'And I'm a man who doesn't allow a woman's whims to influence his decisions. I'm not immune to the ageless urge to possess a beautiful woman, either.'

'You're just unwilling to marry them.'

'That I cannot do.'

'Why not?' She stared deeply into his eyes. Such beautiful eyes! It was like falling into a sparkling pool.

'I was devastated by the loss of my mother. How's that? Is that want you want to hear, Miss Amateur Psychoanalyst?'

'They do say we never entirely escape the trauma of our childhood. I think you associate love with pain.'

'Really?' He leaned forward and, before she knew what he was about, he kissed her mouth hard. 'I'd be happy to discuss this in bed.'

The swift colour gleamed on her creamy skin. 'I'd expect you to do that all the time.'

'And what of your experiences?' he challenged her.

'I spend all my nights by myself.'

His eyes narrowed, became very cynical. 'That sounds unbelievable.'

'It's true.'

'Well who cares?' he said brutally, rising abruptly. 'Work is my birthright. Continuity of the land.'

The thought of spending a whole night with him had stunned Ally to near silence. Obviously, the chemical attraction between them was mutual, drawing them together as strongly as it held them at bay. She touched a finger to her bottom lip, smoothing its cushiony surface.

'Oh, before I forget,' she said raggedly, 'could I ask something very special of you?'

He turned on her, brows beetling. 'If it's to have Keppler out here, skip it.'

'Leon Keppler never crossed my mind. But it's possible it mightn't be such a bad idea. No, I was wondering if you could take Mrs Tanner up in the Beech Baron?'

He lifted a weary hand to his brow. 'God almighty!' he said

said tightly. 'Don't you think joy-rides are a bit much?'

'She has this fear of flying.'

'I had no idea!' His white teeth snapped.

'Please, Kiall.' She decided to risk touching his arm. 'She wants so much to visit her daughter and grandchildren in New Zealand, but up until now she's been terrified of getting on a plane.'

'And she told you all this?'

'Correct.' Ally nodded her head emphatically.

'You're quite a girl. What my foreman calls a dynamite little lady.'

'He said that of me?'

'My God, it's not news to you?'

'Please, I beg you, could you follow this up? She admires you so much. She's feel so safe with you, you could overcome her fears immediately. There's not much future for her if the only people she loves live in another country and she's frightened to visit them.'

'Why don't they come and visit her?' he asked sarcastically.

'Money doesn't mean anything to you. I don't imagine they've got much.'

'Let me think about it,' he said impatiently. 'I do have a trip to do.'

'Thank you, Kiall,' she sighed deeply. 'You've got a heart as big as the whole outdoors.'

'You know what I'd really like?' Ally said, one morning at breakfast. Kiall's presence, a rarity, might have had a good deal to do with her sense of buoyancy and playfulness.

'Do tell us,' he answered, with so much indulgence that an unhappy, brooding expression fell on Karen's face.

'I would simply love to spend a night under the stars.' She smiled at everyone around the table, but Sacha gave an unbelieving moan.

'That's no way to go, Ally. There's no place as comfortable as your own bed.'

'I don't care how uncomfortable it is. I know I'd love it. Please, Kiall.' She touched his wrist. 'I've never seen the stars so big and brilliant as they are out here. A skyful of the most fantastic jewels. I adore the magic of the bush, the smell of the wind and the trees; the way the valleys plunge and the mountains rear out of grasslands. It's like the most marvellous flight from civilisation. I only wish I could ride well enough to go out on a round-up—muster, or whatever.'

Karen's expression was one of displeasure. 'I've been riding since I was three years old,' she contributed coldly.

'Aren't you lucky you didn't get bow legs?'

'You have a positive knack for saying the wrong thing.' Karen flushed.

'Oh, come on, Karen, that's a bit much.'

Susan smiled nervously, looking from one girl to the other. 'I must say your talk with Mrs Tanner had done wonders, Ally,' she said, in an attempt to ease the situation. There's truly been a great improvement. This bacon omelette is delicious.'

'All it needed was a few suggestion,' Ally confirmed modestly. 'We all get stuck in a routine. I knew Mrs Tanner could make wonderful bread and scones, so we just included the brioches and croissants. Don't they just melt in your mouth? It will take weeks for me to lose the weight I've put on.'

'What rubbish!' Sacha said enviously. 'You haven't put on a pound. It makes me absolutely livid! When I remember what the meals were like before and what they're like now, I don't know if I'm going to thank you.'

'Well, I shall,' Kiall said with some feeling. 'The "no time for breakfast" wasn't such a good idea. I find the day goes a whole lot easier when I actually sit down and have something substantial. Especially when it's as well prepared as this. It used to be a couple of cups of black coffee and toast on the run.'

'Now you have a fair idea of the joys of being happily married,' Ally quipped. 'You could even help the little woman set the table.'

'Why would Kiall or "the little woman"—dreadful expression—have to do that?' Karen asked superciliously. 'Obviously you're not familiar with our way of life. My parents have a superb housekeeper.'

'At this rate, our Mrs Tanner might reach her,' Ally replied good-humouredly. 'I quite agree one should get into the habit of consulting with the cook. Enthusiasm on both sides works wonders. Mrs Tanner was especially pleased when Susan went in to talk to her. Still, one likes to do little things oneself. I've been setting the table, in case you haven't noticed.'

'I thought it looked terribly elegant,' Kiall mocked.

'I'm also responsible for the little posies of flowers,' she told him. 'Don't tell me you don't enjoy it. I've been running out into the garden very early.'

'I just didn't know you were so domesticated,' Sacha smiled. 'I supposed you never lifted a finger to do anything.'

'And me born on a farm?' Ally stared at her over the rim of her teacup.

'Have you had a chance to check your mail, Sacha?' Karen interrupted abruptly. 'I thought I spotted Leon Keppler's writing.'

Sacha threw her napkin down. 'Karen, you're the end!' she breathed with deep disgust.

'Was there anything from Keppler?' Kiall asked, his handsome face darkened.

'Yes, of course there was,' Sacha said gruffly, looking towards her mother for support.

'Kiall, dear . . . ' Susan managed hesitantly. From looking

happy and relaxed, she now looked distressed.

'Why not invite him out?' Ally suggested softly.

'I would expect you to say that,' Karen challenged Ally in icy tones.

'I'm the only one who hasn't met him.'

'Do you mind, Ally?' Kiall said decisively, turning his head and giving Ally a quelling stare.

'Yes, I do,' Ally said promptly.

'I don't believe this,' he said in a low voice.

'Try to. It's a dreadful thing to forbid Sacha to see someone.'

'What business is this of yours?' Karen flashed.

'Sacha calls me her friend.'

'Don't you think you're overstepping the mark?'

'How is it you do it all the time?' Ally responded tartly.

'I love him, Kiall,' Sacha cried in a emotional voice.

'Oh, rubbish!' He looked hard and formidable.

'He's probably got a criminal record,' Karen declared.

'I take it you don't like him?' Ally asked.

'I stand by Kiall.'

'That's lousy! Haven't you got a mind of your own?' Ally challenged.

'Let's leave this for now,' Kiall ordered, getting up from the table and giving every appearance of being an angry man. 'I have people flying in this morning.'

'I'll come with you.' The petite Karen actually heaved herself to her feet.

'Don't you find that tiresome?' Ally asked Kiall in an earnest sort of voice. 'You strike me as the sort of man who doesn't like a woman underfoot.'

'Watch yourself, Ally,' he said in a clipped voice.

'I wouldn't dare speak to Kiall the way you do,' Karen declared. 'Only, you're a guest here . . . '

'Why does Kiall put up with her?' Ally asked after they had gone. 'Why does anyone put up with her? She's such an unpleasant creature.'

'She's not to him.'

'Maybe,' Ally was forced to acknowledge, 'but leaving me out, and I'm not important, she has absolutely no right to question you—and in your own home!'

'She's always been like that,' Susan said sadly.

'Hell, you should meet her mother!' Sacha said disgustedly.

'I'm absolutely terrified of Mrs Fulbrook,' Susan confirmed unnecessarily. 'She has always made me feel an outsider. The sort of woman who would never fit in.'

'Have some more tea,' Ally suggested soothingly. 'There's plenty left.'

'I will have another, Ally, dear.' Susan passed her cup. 'It's such a comfort having you here. I knew the moment you arrived you'd get everything moving.'

'I'd like to get Karen moving,' Ally declared. 'I'd enjoy that very much.'

'Everyone wants to know when they're getting married,' Susan said, taking a deep, shuddery breath.

'Good grief, is Kiall hiding a mad passion?' Ally felt her heart rock.

'In some ways, they're very well suited,' Sacha said frowningly.

'You think so?' Ally looked amazed.

'You haven't seen her in company,' Susan supplied. 'Her sort of company. Kiall's sort of company. We've had hundreds of people here from time to time. Important people. When she wants to be, Karen can be very charming. As well, everyone knows her, her family. She's rich. She's very good-looking and very well informed. She loves station life, she was reared to it. She worships Kiall and, what is more, she has waited patiently until every other woman has dropped out of his life.'

'She gave one or two stragglers the old heave-ho,' Sacha added bluntly. 'Kiall has to marry some time. It's important to the station. Mowana.'

'Of course,' Ally nodded. 'This house has the feel of generations. But surely he could have anyone he wanted?'

'I can promise you, he and Karen were very close at one time. Actually, she's not always so unpleasant, although I've never found her nice. It's you she's jealous of. She nearly goes off her rocker if Kiall so much as smiles at another woman, and he laughs at you a lot.'

'He does?'

'You know he does, Ally. Sometimes he tries not to, but his sense of humour is always there. You're good fun, Ally. Karen is not.'

'Gosh, I think she's poisonous!'

Sacha didn't laugh. 'Mum and I are wondering what you think of Kiall.'

Ally paused in shock. Should she really say what she thought, or make a joke? 'He's so darn powerful, he'd loosen a girl's fillings,' she said finally.

'Seriously, Ally.'

'Hey, listen you two——' Ally looked from mother to daughter '—Don't stare at me with identical saucer eyes.'

'I thought there was something a whole lot stronger than liking between you two,' Sacha suggested.

'Who says he likes me?' Ally declared.

'God!' Sacha picked up and drained off a whole cup of tea. 'What about all the riding lessons? He gives them himself. He could ask a dozen hands. All the trips around the station? All the time he's spent with you at the stud-farm? He's never had breakfast with us before, no matter what his explanation, and now he always lingers after dinner.'

'It's not his kind of thing?' Ally asked wryly, busying herself with folding her pale blue damask napkin.

'He likes you, Ally,' Sacha said impatiently. 'Believe us. The point is, what do you think about him?'

'He's a dream.' Ally stopped short at this point.

'Agreed.'

'He's the kind of man to tear a woman's heart out, and I'm not looking for trouble.'

'Even I never expected to see you hit it off so well,' Sacha contributed thoughtfully, drumming her pretty fingers on the table.

'Are you trying to matchmake?' Ally gave her a stern look.

'You'd make a stunning couple,' Sacha said simply. 'And *you* would never put Mum out.'

'For goodness' sake, what are you talking about?' Ally asked, showing her unease.

Susan's smile was full of a quiet resignation. 'You don't think Karen would want me here, do you, Ally?'

'My God, you know Kiall,' Ally returned expressively. 'He would never be dictated to by a woman.'

'Then she'd make herself a right pain,' Sacha insisted. 'In fact, I'm sure she'd make life so intolerable, Mum would have to go.'

Ally studied their doleful expressions. 'Look, is it as serious as that?'

'We believe so.' Sacha nodded her soft, curly head. 'We can't get her to go away.'

'Have you suggested her family might be missing her?'

'So we don't have your spirit.'

'I know it's not my business,' Ally turned to Susan, 'but surely your interests were protected in your husband's will?'

Susan stared down at her gold wedding band. 'I'm the same as Sacha. A trust fund was set up. I'll always be comfortable. Of course, if I remarry the money reverts to the estate.'

'So Kiall inherited everything?'

'Lock, stock and barrel. Understandable. The only son. The only one capable of carrying on a Herculean task.'

'It sounds unfair to me.' Ally scrutinised Susan's passive

face. 'As his widow . . . '

'Don't worry, Ally,' Susan consoled her. 'I have perfect trust in Kiall, but as you know he's gone from daylight to dark. I don't think I'd care to share even this huge house with Karen, and I know her mother wouldn't take long to suggest I find myself somewhere else.'

Ally put her elbows on the table and buried her head in her hands. 'Actually, another place might be the answer,' she said finally, lifting her glowing head. 'I think your life could do with a nice change. Perhaps six months in the city? You've told me yourself you're not a bred-in-the-bone country woman.'

'Mum has never really adapted,' Sacha agreed.

'So there would be tons to do in the city. You could get yourself some marvellous penthouse, perhaps. Something overlooking Sydney harbour. It's glorious! We could go shopping. We could really let our heads go. You're a very pretty woman, Susan. City make-up and dressing would transform you.'

'You think so?' Susan smiled, but her expresssion was wondering.

'I know so. Remember, beauty is my business.'

Susan stared back at Ally wistfully, then her eyes began to twinkle. 'You're a very positive person, aren't you?'

'The definitive Leo.' Ally pulled her hair around her like a mane.

'Why not, with that splendid colouring? I'm fascinated with the way you keep coming up with things. You know, sometimes I think I could look a lot better in the right clothes.'

'Well, you can't just sit here thinking about it and counting all your money,' Ally told her. 'Why don't you come back with me when I go? We could have a marvellous time touring the shops, and I know just the hairdresser for you. You and Sacha have such good hair, and he did wonders for me. I see your hair, Susan, short and winging up around your head. It has such a neat shape.'

Sacha smiled, but without much mirth. 'I know you could do wonders for Mum, Ally, but what about me? I'll go nuts if I don't see Leon.'

'You heard Kiall bite my head off,' Ally told her wryly. 'His eyes go from sparkly lakes to cold steel.'

'He can be tough all right,' Sacha said feelingly. 'What did Leon ever do to outrage him?'

'Obviously he believes your Leon to be a fortune-hunter.'

Sacha sighed. 'Leon's no fortune-hunter. He would love me if I sold cheeseburgers.'

'Are you sure of that?'

'Of course, Ally,' Sacha looked at her friend pleadingly. 'You've got Mrs Tanner eating out of your hand, and she's a pretty tough old bird; can't you speak to Kiall? Convince him that I'm desperately serious, and so is Leon? I swear I'll run away if he forbids me to see Leon. Let's face it, I do have money.'

'What was your opinion of Leon, Susan?'

Susan squeezed her hands together, looking nervous of answering. 'He's very charming. Very smooth. Very well spoken.'

'You could sound a bit more enthusiastic, Mum!' Sacha cried wrathfully. 'Anyway, you always side with Kiall.'

'Sacha, darling, you're my daughter!' Susan sounded unhappy and pressurised. 'You're everything in life to me. Your happiness is paramount.'

'Then why won't you back me over Leon?'

'It seemed to me, darling, he was a little old for you,' Susan sounded out tentatively.

'What, ten years?' Sacha scoffed. 'You know I like an older man. Besides, he has to be older to be successful in his own right.'

'Is that the only objection, Susan?' Ally asked.

'It's so difficult, isn't it, assessing people's true motives?' Susan's blue gaze shied away. 'I must say, he seems very attached to Sacha.'

'Attached?' Sacha made a sound of complete disgust. 'He's *mad* for me. On fire!'

'Well, that sounds incendiary enough!' Ally made a determined effort to lighten the atmosphere. 'I suppose I could find a quiet moment with Kiall. It will have to be way out in the bush. Karen patrols the corridors.'

'He'll listen to you,' Sacha urged.

'That's news to me, but for your sake I'll have a try.'

Ally, though making great progress, didn't feel up to taking the plunge on horseback across the rugged savannahs. She took the Land Cruiser instead. Red dust flew up from the tracks. Horses galloped along white-railed boundaries, several the pure white of fairy-tales, cattle looked up to stare at her and millions of birds exploded from the trees, forming a palette of jewel colours: ruby, emerald, garnet, sapphire, canary diamonds. She was having a marvellous time at the wheel, her long hair tied back by a silk scarf, executing a lot of hair-pin turns and avoiding the pot-holes. She had been told by Charlie, an ancient aboriginal who liked painting in the garden, that Mr Kiall was cross-country at the Twelve Mile. Some of the men were working there. She had to avoid Coorie creek at all costs. Mowana was having intermittent visitations from the rain god, and no one but a local could expect to know just how quickly the water courses could rise. Ally decided to bypass it altogether. No water-crossing for her, though she was revelling in the gradients. What she didn't realise was that Mowana was criss-crossed by water-holes and swamps that, in downpours, could turn into billabongs and deep lagoons.

She was intoxicated by the beauty of her surroundings, its

vast lushness, mile upon mile. The savannahs were covered with thick spear grass, whose colours turned from flaxen to jade overnight; the purple moutains looked remarkable; and wild flowers in great profusion and variety spangled the unparalled vistas. A sheet of still, emerald-green water glowed to the right of her. Its surface was studded by pink waterlilies of fantastic size. Some five miles away, cattle were grazing in their thousands, and it was then she decided on taking a short-cut. The Land Cruiser was a stout vehicle, and she didn't have all that much time before dusk set in. Karen had returned to the house to work on making herself beautiful for dinner. Two of Kiall's important male visitors were staying on overnight.

She had perhaps ten minutes of high adventure until, rocketing over a rosy red hill, she came down almost immediately on a freshly watered bog-hole.

'You'll make it!' she urged the gallant Land Crusier. Oh, surely four-wheel drives could go anywhere? But the bog-hole was so deep that to her horror, water flowed across the bonnet as she ploughed in. Old Charlie had never told her about this! If the water-hole had been any bigger, she thought, she would have floated away. Who knew *what* it would look like in the Wet? Probably as big as a crocodile pad.

Put to the test, instead of ploughing out of trouble, the vehicle settled firmly in the mud and then played dead. With the water lapping the sides, Ally didn't dare open the door, but had to consider leaving by the window. She didn't have much alternative. As far as she knew, the winch was on the bumper-bar, and that was now well submerged. Even if she could get to it, she thought, the most substantial-looking tree was well out of range. There was more to communing with nature than innocent pleasure. She only hoped that, apart from being bogged, she hadn't damaged the vehicle. It was her one and only experience of driving in a mud-pond.

She flinched when she sank into the dank, muddy water.

Oh, what a feeling it was to have mud ooze into one's shoes! Her sporty cotton shirt with its interesting shoulder and pocket treatment was now splattered with huge ochre dots, her narrow cotton slacks were surely ruined, but apart from that she had sustained no damage. There was no reason why she couldn't get herself out of this mess. On the other hand, women could be brave but they weren't terribly mechanical. She had her eye on a gum tree now, but as she tried to wade towards it the mud began to play terrible tricks, closing around her ankles and holding her in a vice. She was unable to move!

Like many another alone and in a predicament she began to talk to herself.

'Don't panic, girl!' Despite that, she wrenched her ankle as she tried to drag herself out. Tears came into her eyes. 'Damn!' She had visions of a hand waving above quicksand.

She leaned nearer the Land Cruiser and got a grip on the door, manoeuvring laboriously until she almost had herself out. Only then could she afford to laugh. The first step was losing her shoes, sandals certainly, but quite expensive. Still, it was exquisite to be free. She hauled herself up, then climbed on to the bonnet and from there slithered across the hood to the rear of the vehicle, descending by the spare tyre.

When she reached the dry, higher grade she looked down at herself. Bushwhacked, she thought wryly, and you've no one to blame but yourself.

She lost count of the birds who came to see what was happening. One tree was so covered with white corellas, it looked as if it was decorated with great white flowers. Afternoon sunlight danced through the shining leaves and Ally jumped back in fright and astonishment as a huge monitor lizard materialised from a fallen log, head and shoulders raised by its forelegs, staring at her. It was about four feet in length, with a ridged and powerful tail, a truly bizarre sight.

To Ally's city eyes it looked incredibly dangerous. If it

decided to attack her, she thought, she was in big trouble, but there she was wrong. The goanna was as stupefied to see her as she was to see it. The two of them stood motionless, Ally preparing to made a determined leap up a tree. But, grotesque as it looked, the lizard was evidently friendly, or she didn't inspire fear. It peered at her for a few moments longer, seemed to wink playfully, then turned and made slow, dignified progress back into the bush.

Another experience she had never had before! Ally swallowed to relieve her parched throat, and only then did it occur to her there was a transceiver in the vehicle. She could call the station—always supposing the transceiver was still working. Obviously, she had to be rescued. Or she could walk and the four-wheel drive could be rescued. She had the feeling the winch line would only make it three-quarters of the way to the nearest stout tree, and in any case she wasn't at all sure what she was supposed to do. Karen would be the genius there. Karen would never have allowed herself to sink into mud.

It was surprising how much it took out of her, crawling back into the Cruiser. Her legs seemed to be rubbery. Another few anxious moments of crackle and she was through to the station

A voice answered her. 'Is there anything you wish to say?'

'Karen?' Ally asked, startled. What was Karen doing in the radio room?

'Try to relay your message,' Karen urged coldly. 'I don't have all night.'

'Thanks a lot.' Ally put out her plea for rescue. 'Try to make it, won't you?' She signed out. 'It's getting on for dusk here.'

She wouldn't be hard to find, she consoled herself afterwards. Unless Karen didn't bother to tell anybody. Ally grinned to herself. Karen was one prickly lady, but she wouldn't do that. Personal likes and dislikes couldn't be allowed to hinder rescues.

A good half-hour went past, and the golden-green air was turning a misty blue. I'll call again, she thought, and immediately decided against it. She could hardly expect someone to be ready on the spot. Another half-hour and she was certain something was wrong. She had said something about sleeping under the stars, now it seemed she was going to get her wish! She tried to start the vehicle again, but it was completely immobilised. It was anything but exciting to have the two front wheels buried deep in the mud.

The most frustrating thing was, the next time she tried the transceiver, she couldn't raise anyone. What the heck was going on? She knew she had left the main track—she now supposed that was a big no-no—but Kiall would know Mowana like the back of his hand. She hadn't headed off into complete wilderness.

Twenty minutes later, as Ally was trying desperately to drive all thought of snakes from her mind, dazzling lights pierced the inky blackness.

Someone was coming for her, thank God! For the past hour she had become terribly aware of bush aloneness. It was an eerie feeling, the least sound making the hair stand up on the nape of her neck. It had begun to dawn on her what it was like to be hopelessly lost. The ageless bush was magnificent, but in different circumstances it could be pitiless and desolate. Stories abounded of travellers who had been found too late, or not found at all. She made the decision she would always look before she leapt. Since she had been bogged, she had also discovered her track petered out less than a hundred yards ahead, going nowhere.

A far more experienced person than she brought his vehicle to a halt at the crest of the steep grade. The brilliance of the driving-lights, supplementing the main beams, pierced the darkness, enabling the driver to see all before him. In an instant night turned to day and Ally began to lever herself out of the driving-seat and on to the raised section of the bonnet. The odour of dankness and mud clung to it, and the peculiar greenness of the bush seemed to fill the air.

'Ally?'

It was Kiall's voice, hard and imperious.

'I'm here.' She scrambled across the hood, and as she did so he leapt down the hill and hauled her on to the dry, rugged track.

Despite the pain of being manhandled, a tremendous relief flared in her. 'When your world falls apart, call for Lancaster,' she quipped.

'Just a minute,' he bit off harshly. 'Are you all right?'

'Oh course I'm all right. I made it out of the mud. The ole vee-hicle didn't.'

'I'm not surprised, when you know nothing about them.'

She stared up at his taut face. 'Take it easy now, Mr Lancaster. I don't like to get blasted.'

'I'm not going to apologise, you need it,' he told her shortly. 'I have a very personal interest in my guests. I don't like them haring around at night. When we heard nothing from you, we naturally got anxious.'

'Anxious, angry, which is it?' She tried to free herself, but he held her firmly.

'Both.'

'Well, I've some news to pass on. I spoke to Karen a good hour and half ago. I told her almost exactly where I was.'

His face took on a disturbing expression. 'You just made that up.'

'What?' She glared at him, then had to glance down feverishly at her foot. 'Something crawled over me.'

'Oh? You're wearing no shoes.'

'They're back there in the mud.'

'I half expected you'd be there to join them.' Kiall looked frowningly over her head. 'Nothing else to do but leave the

Cruiser there. We'll have to winch it out in the morning.'

'I'm truly sorry.' Ally clicked her tongue.

'You sound it.'

'How do you want me to sound?' she demanded in a sudden fury. 'I don't go for that machismo stuff, you know.'

'And women that come on too strong I usually tell to get lost.'

'I did get lost,' she started in fiery tones, then suddenly laughed. 'I got lost. I got muddied up. I lost expensive shoes. I had a confrontation with a giant goanna, and waking nightmares about snakes. I need to wash my hair and take a hot shower.'

'You're making it sound very attractive.' He took her arm and all but hauled her up the hill. 'I had to walk out on my guests.'

'For little old me?' Her hair, freed of the scarf, tumbled about her face.

'I checked the main track before trying here,' he told her, sounding irritated.

'I figured you would. In some ways, I like your style.'

'Well, I'm not exactly thrilled with you. You've only been here about ten days, and you've turned the whole place upside-down.'

'That gives you a good excuse not to have me back. Ouch!' she wailed as her right foot struck a rock.

'What's the matter now?' His eyes drilled a hole through her.

'I think I've broken my toe.'

'How?' Concern mixed with impatience. 'We'd better have a look at it.'

'You'd never see it. It's plastered in mud.'

'Do you want to get in the Merc?' He indicated the big four-wheel drive.

'Sure. I suppose if I'd have taken this you would have killed me.'

'You're so right,' he admitted. 'Climb in . . . be careful,' he admonished swiftly, as her foot slipped and she fell back against him.

'Remind me never to take a mud-bath,' she chuckled drily. 'I have to say, it's unusual seeing you such a mess!'

'Don't worry, I'll make myself nice with a shower.'

'Anyway, you're still worth nibbling.' Treacherously, his arms closed around her waist and he lowered his head, his teeth catching the silky lobe of her ear.

'That's sweet of you, but it's been a long day!'

'You were the one who started this "live a little", ' he taunted her.

She tried to shrug it off, but her body was suddenly shaking, transformed in an instant to a column of pure sensation. It simply wasn't like her to race headlong into danger. 'It's getting late, Kiall,' she said, her voice dropping to a husky whisper.

He ignored that, wrapping her more tightly into his arms. 'Probably someone else would have taken twice as long to find you.' His mouth moved down the creamy curve of her neck, igniting a firestorm. 'I'm two people when I'm with you. One wants to beat you, the other wants to make love to you. Very thoroughly.'

Unconsciously Ally was insinuating her body against his, enmeshed in sensation. 'Except you're rumoured to be involved with another woman.' Her mind was striving desperately to distance itself from what was happening to her body.

'Why, Ally,' his voice came to her, low and mocking, 'I didn't think things like that made you fall apart.'

Her lids, that had been falling languorously, snapped back. She had to be mad to cede control to the man! 'Does that mean what I think it does?'

He laughed gently, his hand lifting the heavy, silken slide of her hair. 'All I know is, you have the most incredible skin. It's so luscious, you're edible.'

'And Karen isn't?'

'No, you're the only one.' His hands moved to beneath her breasts, and immediately she tried to twist away, as a searing wildness overtook her. So powerful was his effect on her, she was shuddering when she was barely touched.

'I'd like to kill you,' she muttered, emotions building like a storm.

'It seems we threaten one another.'

'Kiall, you'll have to stop.' She got a very firm grip on his controlling arms, feeling the strength of bone and muscle beneath the sleek veil of sun-coppered skin.

'All right,' he relented. 'Turn around and let me kiss you. Just once.'

'Absolutely not!' she exploded.

'You have my word. Just once. When you call for Lancaster, you have to be prepared to pay.'

Something within her rose up to challenge him. 'Provided it's just a kiss, OK. I have very strong views about sexual harassment.'

'What's that, you love it?'

'Spoken like a true male!' she cried scornfully, spinning around and pitting the full strength of her slender-boned body against his.

'What is the bottom line?' He wrestled with her almost tenderly.

'I told you. I'm my own woman.'

'What a shame! I'm not sleeping anywhere near as well as I did before you came here.'

'And you think you're on to a brief affair?'

'At least it would be memorable. Spectacular, even.'

'Well, that I cannot do.' She gritted her small teeth. 'I know it must be astonishing for you. You only see women in terms of diversion, but I've a lot more to offer than some meaningless sexual relationship.'

'I can't help feeling that at some level you're offering yourself to me as a wife,' he offered blandly.

She was so angry, she stammered, 'I could never comtemplate anything so horrendous! I'm not going through my life a nothing and a no one, overwhelmed by a male tyrant. I'm a self-governing individual.'

'I guess a man could live with it.' He turned her a little, the better to see her. 'Until it was time to go to bed. Come here to me, Ally.'

Some special nuance in his voice turned her heart over.

'Don't count on my not screaming,' she warned.

'A few miles further in and it might have been a challenge, but as it is . . . ' He bent his head and his hands slid down over her back, sensously tracing its contours. There was a drumming sound in her ears, but as his mouth reached for hers she was overcome by that ineffable melting sensation only he could induce. How could she deny his real power? It wasn't anything as basic as raw sexual attraction. That was something her code of ethics could withstand. It was something very deep and mysterious. Something that, if one was lucky, only came once in a lifetime.

Their mouths met with a sort violence, as though each was straining to capture something vital from the other—some essence of the true self. True passion was as much of the mind as the body, and for Ally it carried the double weight of special vulnerability. She had the tumultuous feeling that what she was offering was irrecoverable.

Her lips felt incredibly tender, sensitive to an almost unbearable degree. She felt as alight as autumn leaves set on fire. His hands had moved to her face now, cupping it, holding it up to him, while somehow, she had no clear recollection, her

own hands were moving over his back, revelling in the tension
of sinew and muscle. He had a superb body and she was
panicked by the thought of having him for a lover. He was so
endlessly powerful. Much as she tried to fight it, a man's sheer
physicality exerted a profound influence. It was as much to be
feared as rejoiced in. A complication of her intense longing was
the grief she would feel if she allowed herself to come to love
him. For her love to be returned was what a woman's
happiness was all about. She fully realised now that she was in
love with him, caught up in his increasingly dominant aura.
Why, the very thought of him filled her days and her nights,
colouring her existence. Here in the wilderness her desire for
him seemed infinite. She was, for the first time in her life,
truly frightened of the pleasure he was giving her, and so
closely were they fused, she seemed to sense an answering
trepidation in him.

The one kiss had spun out into long, open exploration. They
were approaching the stage when kissing, however
passionately, simply wasn't enough. Their coming together
had an undertaste of frenzy. His hand burned over her breast
and she arched, desperate for him to caresss the nipple and
equally desperate to protect one of the most vulnerable areas of
her woman's body.

Unmistakably his thumb worked the peaked nipple, and she
thought eerily that she might be able to do little but give him
what he wanted. She felt an enormous softness, a yielding, and
he responded elementally, lifting her up to him, and pressing
his mouth to the thin cotton that sheathed her urgent flesh.

She couldn't hold still. Couldn't. Yearning was cutting
deeply into her. Yearning she had never been able to imagine
before.

'Hold still,' he said in a deep, drugged tone.

'Kiall . . . *please*.' She knew she sounded young and
frightened, quite unlike herself.

He allowed her feet to touch the ground, and she had to drop her head forward so that it pressed against his chest.

'And this is the girl who knows what affairs are all about?'

'Don't talk rubbish,' she said in an utterly spent tone.

He took a handful of her hair and pulled her head back. 'Are you telling me you haven't had a string of lovers?' He searched her eyes.

'You and your fantasies!' she blazed abruptly. She planted a hand on his hard chest and held herself away from him. 'You don't know the first thing I'm about. You're the one with the terrible reputation. Compared to you, I'm a puritan!' She tried to thrust away from him and almost went flying, sending pebbles bouncing down the hill.

'Take it easy, damn it!' He scooped her up in his intolerable, authoritative fashion.

'*You* take it easy,' she flared. 'I have a great respect for my body. I don't make it available to anyone, and that includes you, Mr Almighty Lancaster.'

'Even when you're fighting me, you somehow seem defenceless,' he gritted.

'That's because you're a brute. No one would be happy taking on a man of six foot four.'

'Might I remind you you've got a few more extra inches than most people yourself.'

'Well, I'm not responsible for that!' she protested, promising herself some karate lessons.

'Listen, settle down,' he urged her. 'I don't enjoy using extra muscle, though it comes in handy. Occasionally. Like now.'

'This thing is getting undignified,' Ally admitted as he released her. She rubbed her smarting arms. 'Do you think we could possibly go home? Everyone will want to know how I managed to get myself all done up for a corroboree.'

'Aboriginal you ain't,' he corrected her satirically. 'Any self-respecting lubra knows how to keep her place.'

CHAPTER FIVE

THEY were all stationed on the veranda: Susan, Sacha, a very severe-looking Karen, even Mrs Tanner, twisting her pristine apron into anxious knots.

'Thank God, Ally!' Susan came towards her, holding out her arms. She seemed completely undeterred by Ally's bedraggled appearance. 'We were so worried, you have no idea!'

'Don't get excited.' Ally greeted her gently. 'I was safe.'

'Where did you get to, girl?' Sacha asked, clamping an encouraging hand on Ally's shoulder.

'Ask Karen. I gave her fairly precise directions,' Ally said smartly.

'You did *what*?' Karen's small features froze.

'What did you think you were supposed to do, keep it all to yourself?'

'I have no idea what you're talking about,' Karen answered with frigid dignity. 'I was as anxious as anyone.'

Susan was quite as a loss to follow the two girls' exchange. 'You'll want to get into a nice hot tub, Ally,' she interrupted soothingly.

'That I will. Hello, Mrs Tanner!'

The housekeeper was standing, looking solemn, and Ally smiled at her. 'If you don't ask, you'll never know. I drove the Land Cruiser into a bog-hole. One moment I was swooping over a hill, the next I was up to my knees in mud.'

'And your shoes?' So much for her foolishness, Ally thought; Mrs Tanner actually looked amused.

'I decided to write them off.'

Karen shook her dark, gleaming head in mock amazement. 'Very plainly, you shouldn't be let out by yourself.'

'At least I'll know not to SOS *you* in future,' Ally said.

'What was that all about?' Sacha asked in the privacy of Ally's bedroom. She sat on the four-poster while Ally stripped off her clothes in the adjoining bathroom.

'I called in the station about dusk. Karen answered.'

'Really?' Sacha sounded shocked.

'If you don't mind! I certainly did.'

'She never said a word.'

'I can understand why.' Ally studied her face in the mirror. 'She was hoping someone would have to pick me up tomorrow morning. You obviously know nothing about my mental resources. Nothing scares me. Snakes, maybe. They've a bit shattering.'

'What did Kiall say?' Sacha called.

'Ask a silly question . . . ' Ally wrapped a large fleecy towel around her. 'As a long-standing friend, he felt it incumbent upon him to defend Karen's honour. He accused me of making it up.'

'I suppose he couldn't believe she was rotten enough to do it,' Sacha declared, wide-eyed.

'But *I* was rotten enough to lie?'

'Fancy that!' Sacha shook her pretty head. 'He got going on a search pretty smartly. He's never a slow move but, boy, he was flying! If I didn't know better, I would have said he was agitated. I wouldn't care to be in Karen's shoes when he finds out *she* was lying.'

'Well, he won't find out any more from me. I propose to drop it,' Ally said.

'You've got to take her seriously, Ally,' Sacha warned. 'If her jealousy turns out to be too much, Mum will have to ask her to go.'

'Her jealousy doesn't depress me.' Ally padded towards her

friend and gave her a big hug. 'Hop out of here, kiddo, while I take a shower.'

'You know Gerald Owens and Major Dawson are staying over?'

'Good. Glad to hear it,' Ally said. 'I rather thought Susan had a little fondness for Major Dawson.'

'Since when?' Sacha turned to stare at Ally with a look of amazement.

'What's so disturbing about that?' Ally returned directly.

'Gosh, Ally, Mum is pushing forty-two!'

'Sure she is! The prime of life. Let me refresh your memory. Joan Collins and Liz Taylor are in their fifties. Audrey Hepburn, Lollobrigida, heaps of others. All that stuff about being over the hill should be dumped. A woman can be attractive as long as she wants. All she has to do is put in a little work.'

'Well, you're wrong about Mum.'

'Am I?' Ally said.

A student of body language, Ally was convinced of her intuition by the time the evening was over. Susan positively blossomed when exposed to the full gallantry of Major Dawson's rather delightfully old-fashioned manner. Ally herself found him a most charming man, full of wit and warmth and sincerity. He was a widower, somewhere in his mid-fifties, distinguished and upstanding in appearance, with a fine shock of prematurely silver hair that contrasted well with thick dark brows, and his grey gaze, though searching, was unquestionably kind. One would have to be either stupid or blind, Ally considered, not to notice that he felt a certain *tendresse* for the shy and modest Susan. Their bodies actually inclined towards each other, his silver head tipped protectively, her small hand fluttering, but never touching, and Ally found the whole spectacle fascinating. Susan deserved a bit of cherishing, she thought. Her unhappy marriage had left a stamp on her, but Ally fervently hoped it wouldn't be indelible. Sacha seemed to think her mother's best time was over. Ally preferred to think that Susan, with just a little gentle prodding, could come into her own. By comparision, Gerald Owens was rather stiff and formal. Both men were pastoralists with a special interest in horses, particularly Arabs. Major Dawson had at one time been a brilliant polo player with an international reputation, and it was he who claimed over dinner that he could coach Kiall to greatness if only Kiall could overcome his killing work-load.

'Your style is effortless, my boy,' Major Dawson enthused. 'All that marvellous strength and power allied to speed and finesse. Players of your calibre don't come along too often, I can tell you. If you hadn't devoted your life to Mowana, I could make you a superemo of the game.'

Kiall inclined his wine-glass. 'The real heroes are the ponies,' he pointed out gently, laughing fame off.

'Isn't there a polo field here?' Ally asked with interest, her beautiful eyes glowing. She was wearing another of her so-simple, superbly cut dinner dresses in bronze and white printed silk, but she wore her stunning looks with grace and ease. Ally didn't rate her outer self above her inner self, and her friendly, unselfconscious manner helped to make others open up.

'Of course there is!' Susan confirmed, looking at her stepson with pride and affection. 'Why don't you arrange a match, Kiall, while Ally is here? It would be lovely if you could be here when that happened, Tom. You too, of course, Gerald.'

'Sterling idea,' Major Dawson gently applauded. 'I know for sure all the girls adore "Lord" Lancaster.'

'There's no other player to match Kiall.' Karen gave her host a burning, possessive glance.

'And it is marvellous to be superbly mounted,' Gerald

Owens observed enviously. 'My own boy is a real bulldog. You'll include him in the team, of course, Kiall?'

'Bound to. Pete is tireless,' Kiall returned smoothly.

So it was arranged. Two teams would be assembled by the weekend after next.

'We'll have a party as well,' Sacha cried delightedly. 'Invite a whole crowd.'

That crowd meant Leon Keppler, Ally felt sure.

Ally was retiring for bed after an eventful day when a knock came on her door. Probably Sacha, wanting to know if she had had a chance to speak to Kiall. Ally shouldered into her satin *peignoir* and walked to the door.

'Could I speak to you for a few moments?' Karen Fulbrook demanded the instant they were face to face.

Ally stood back. 'I certainly would like to know why you didn't relay my message for help.'

'To be quite honest, it went clear out of my mind.' Karen prowled around the room, giving every appearance of checking whether Ally had carelessly damaged the precious furnishings.

'Unreal.'

'I assure you, it did.' Karen's dark eyes flashed. 'I do wish you would sit down. I detest people looming over me.'

'Haven't you got a footstool at your place?'

'I beg your pardon?' Karen's delicate black brows drew together.

'Well, if you carried one around you could be certain of equality.'

'I was really hoping you wouldn't joke.'

'I'm sorry.' Ally pressed her lips together. 'Please sit down, Karen.' She indicated an armchair. 'What would you like to talk about?'

For an instant, Karen surrendered herself to the past. She tilted her pointed chin, staring around the room. 'This was

Kiall's mother's room, you know.'

Ally nodded. 'He told me.'

'I marvel he allowed you to use it.'

'So do I. He had a lot of others to choose from.'

'I don't remember the first Mrs Lancaster,' Karen said sombrely. 'Some people say the only Mrs Lancaster, but my mother said she was the most dazzling creature she had ever laid eyes on. No one likes to talk about anything else but her charm and beauty, the authority she had as mistress of this house. Her morals, of course, were quite disgraceful.'

'As you didn't know her, how are you in any position to judge?'

'I've just told you,' Karen said shortly. 'She ran off and left her husband. Left her only child.'

'Maybe she was terribly unhappy,' Ally pondered. 'I'm not making excuses, neither am I going to judge.'

'Well, I can tell you Kiall has no time for the enchantresses of this world. The heartless sirens!' Karen fairly blazed.

'He told me so himself.' Ally nodded imperturbably.

Karen shrugged her doll-like shoulders, covered in aquamarine lace. 'The way I heard it, he doesn't think much of you.'

Ally looked at the older girl long and thoughtfully. 'You love Kiall, don't you?'

'I'd be happy to die for him,' Karen declared.

'How staggering! I can understand a parent dying for a child, but I don't think I would like to be called on to commit hari-kari for a man.'

'Kiall is my life,' Karen retorted fiercely.

'I suppose women in love tend to see their men like that. Have you never thought of a little self-definition?'

'What do you mean?'

'There doesn't seem much point in allowing Kiall to become such an obsession. Why doesn't he offer matrimony?

Surely that's natural when people are in love and there's nothing to stop it. You've known Kiall most of your life. You must be what—twenty-six, twenty-seven?'

'Twenty-eight, if you must know, but I don't look anything like it.'

'Take it easy. Being twenty-eight isn't going into a decline. Why do we women have this obsession with age? Does a woman only live until she's thirty?'

'Those are generally accepted to be her best years.'

'For whom? Do you see yourself as a sex-symbol?'

'I'm sure you do.' The small, high-bred face looked inexpressibly haughty.

'As a matter of fact, I don't. I have a different perception of myself altogether. What I'm trying to say is this: if these are your best years, and I don't agree, why are you wasting them on a man who simply won't come to the altar? Isn't that an indication he doesn't truly love you? He only wants to use you.'

'My dear Miss Allen,' Karen drew a shuddery breath, 'I know all your feminist arguments are merely a means to an end. You want him yourself.'

Ally's gold-starred eyes sparkled with intelligence and compassion. 'I find him extremely attractive, as you might as well know.'

'Oh, I do. I do!' Karen laughed bitterly.

'But he's a risk. A very high risk.'

'Isn't any man who's dangerous and exciting?' Karen retorted a little wildly.

'Well, those adjectives describe him, but I've long since trained myself out of playing with fire. Kiall Lancaster is no ordinary flame, but a raging bushfire.'

'So how do you know?' The veneer of civility, always thin, cracked wide open, and terror and hostility stared out of Karen's pale bedtime face.

'I'm not sure I *do* know,' Ally said equably. 'I'm guessing.'

'You'd better be.' The cameo face was made ugly by jealousy. 'He's mine, and I won't let you have him!'

'Can't I speak to you woman to woman?' Ally said quietly. 'I just told you I haven't put in a bid. It's not in me, Karen, to go completely overboard. I'm not the woman for obsession. I don't like talking about my host, either, as though he were a prize stallion. You call me a feminist; by that, *I* mean championing the right of women to develop fully, instead of living in a man's shadow. I'm still woman enough to allow a man the traditional sexual role. As far as I'm concerned, the man can do the running. If the man I cared about didn't want me as I wanted him, I think I'd have to take it on the chin. I can't be sure, I've never been tested. But start thinking, what it would be like to be married to a man who didn't really love you. Who married you because you fitted his life-style. You must realise that all your devotion isn't being returned.'

'Keep on saying it, but it's not true. Kiall loves me,' Karen protested, looking curiously fragile.

'Then don't take a back seat,' Ally advised. 'Start laying down the law. It's not very clever, allowing him to keep you on the hook. Start writing out wedding invitations and see what happens.

'You think you know so much.' Karen rose to her feet, the veneer of civility settled back in place. 'You know nothing about Kiall and me. As you say, you're the ordinary person, we are not.'

'If that's the case, I appreciate being ordinary,' Ally returned wryly. 'The way our men treat us is determined by the way we allow them to treat us. I'll admit they've been conditioned over thousands of years to look on us like children, so sometimes it's not easy to get through. All I can say to you is that, as far as I'm concerned, Kiall is committed to no one. You don't wear a ring on your finger. When you do, I promise I'll be the first to respect it. Right at the moment I'm enjoying myself. Despite all my training, I do have an unruly streak. Put it down to my colouring. I sympathise with you, Karen. Please believe that. I do. But I will not be threatened. You've been extremely unpleasant to me from the moment I arrived. Every time you open your mouth to speak, it's something snide. I refuse to allow it to upset me, but you must be aware it's upsetting Susan and Sacha.'

'Both of them, of course, are very much against me.' Karen's small nostrils flared.

'Would you blame them?' Ally asked reasonably. 'I like to think I'm a tolerant woman, but if you treated me the way you treat Susan, I'd bundle you bodily into your little Cessna. I'd even manually start up the propeller! Susan may take it, but I'm sure she finds your patronising manner wounding.'

'And there you have the perfect example of a wimp,' Karen said outrageously. 'When has Susan ever been different? Always cringing and fawning. She tells us all repeatedly that she adores Kiall, and that's good enough reason for his having to put up with her.'

'My goodness, aren't you a wash-out of a guest?' Ally said, for the first time angrily. 'Susan is Kiall's stepmother. She has a very real position in his life. He would be the first to tell you she has always done her best for him.'

'Her best?' Karen sneered contemptuously. 'No one ever did understand just why Kiall's father married her. She's a nothing and a nobody. Always was. Always will be.'

'Get out!' Ally said firmly, a veritable goddess in her anger. 'You offend all decency.'

'You think I don't know what an opportunist you are?' Karen mocked. 'All you're trying to do is get close to the family so you'll have them in there rooting for you in your bid for Kiall. Cross me and you'll be desperately sorry. I am very well known. My family is important, well established in society. You're a common model. Someone who sells her body.'

'You heard me!' Ally said shortly, grasping Karen's arm and giving her the shock of her life. 'Get out of here. I don't want vile people around.'

'Let me go!' Karen wasn't happy about the way she was being moved. It wasn't any scruffy struggle. Ally's lithe, athletic body was part of her business, and she was propelling the petite Karen like a puppet. 'You're a madwoman, do you know that?'

'You don't know how mad, when you insult people I care about.'

'You're bruising me all over.'

'I know.' Just as Ally got a hand on the doorknob, Karen suddenly thought of a great idea. She put back her head, opened her mouth wide and shrieked.

What she really needed was a good smack in the face, but Ally wasn't prepared to go so far. 'Oh, shut up!' she said with complete disgust, but Karen's silvery tones were soaring, deepening into a full-blooded scream.

The girl's a real cuckoo, Ally thought. She remembered something significant her father always said: Never mix with the sillies. Something like that.

Karen had now fallen against the doorjamb, looking so distraught, even Ally was beginning to take her seriously.

Footsteps pounded along the corridor. The first to appear was Kiall, still fully dressed and wearing the expression of a man totally alert to some danger.

'For God's sake, what's going on?' The trigger-alert seemed to relax a little as he saw the two girls standing there.

Immediately, Karen began to babble. 'Kiall, oh, Kiall!' She put out her arms to him as her small, slender frame crumpled dramatically.

'Is she ill?' Kiall shot a silver, sword-like glance at Ally, gathering Karen into his arms and carrying her back into Ally's room.

'She sure is,' Ally answered laconically. She imagined he would deposit Karen on the bed, which she had decided she wouldn't like, but mercifully he put her down on the pink moiré-covered sofa, where she lay back like Camille.

Susan and Sacha rushed in, in their nightclothes, their faces registering alarm.

'I heard screaming,' Susan cried, looking to Ally for reassurance.

'You heard screaming. I heard screaming. It's a good thing Major Dawson and Mr Owens are in the guest wing, or they'd have heard it, too. Karen obviously thinks the best way to get attention is to open her mouth and shriek.'

'What about?' Sacha, who had fallen asleep immediately her head had hit the pillow, was blinking like a small white rabbit.

Karen had started to cry; it was a truly professional piece of acting, or else she was emotionally unstable. 'I only came to say it was cruel of her to make up that story about taking a message from her this afternoon. Of course I didn't. You all know me. I didn't. She never gave me a chance. She has a vicious temper.'

Kiall, who was sitting at Karen's small feet, looked around, his handsome dark face quite menacing. 'What's all this about, Ally?' he clipped off.

Ally shrugged, the light gleaming all over her and firing her hair. 'People often take advantage of my good nature. She's telling a pack of lies. Beyond that I'm pleading the Fifth Amendment.'

'Please, Kiall. Please let me tell you all about it,' Karen implored. In contrast to Ally's superb Junoesque stature, she looked utterly crushable, with the deep V of her nightdress revealing her small breasts and a row of bones like pearl buttons.

'What is this?' Sacha looked both perplexed and disgusted.

She came and stood beside Ally, looking up at Ally's perfect, now implacable profile. At moments like that, one could see Ally had a very firm jawline indeed.

'It's as much a mystery to me as it is to you,' Ally told her wryly. 'I'm the innocent party here.'

'She hit me, would you believe?' Karen wailed in shock.

'She's lying through her teeth.'

'She laid hands on me and thrust me across the room.'

'Talk about the definitive mixed-up kid!'

'Do you like the idea of her pushing me around, Kiall?' Karen begged. 'It's too much, her hostility and insolence. People like her feel they can use physical violence. One can always recognise a lack of breeding.'

'I'd say so.' Ally looked at the older girl with amused contempt. 'It's after twelve. Is anyone going to bed?'

'I'm trying to find out what's been going on here,' Kiall told the defiant Ally very crisply.

'There's nothing to be gained.'

'I'll be the judge of that.'

'You're the boss—right?'

'Ally,' he shook his head, 'you'd try the patience of a saint.'

'And a saint you ain't.'

'I'm going,' Sacha said smartly.

'Let me take you back to your room, dear.' Susan went towards Karen, speaking very kindly.

'Yeah, let Ally and Kiall fight it out,' Sacha began almost blithely.

'Wake up, Susan,' Karen implored her. 'She's an opportunist. Why can't you see that? She's using her friendship with Sacha for her own gain.'

'Now, now, dear,' Susan murmured imperturbably, 'that's simply not true. There's absolutely no way you could diminish Ally in my eyes. Never in my life has any woman, young or old, been so nice to me. I'm not such a fool I don't know who's real.'

'You're blinded by her charm. Why, the things she said!'

'Come, Karen,' Susan said, very firmly for her.

'I've never been so distressed, so shocked in my life.' Karen allowed herself to be assisted to her feet. 'I'm so sorry I got you out of bed. She's just so strong, I was really frightened.'

'Lots of protein,' Ally said. As Susan led Karen away, she reached out and patted the older girl on the head. 'You want to try some. Vitamin B6 might help as well!'

Sacha stood watching for a moment, then burst out laughing. 'You certainly know how to get things moving.'

Ally smiled, but underneath she was upset. 'Any more crazies in her family?'

'When you're finished being flippant,' Kiall said grimly, 'perhaps you'll tell me what was going on.'

'Not if you look like that, I won't.'

'Excuse me, you two!' Sacha cried. 'Maybe if Karen's so distressed she might fly off and we'll never see her again.'

Ally stared after Sacha's departing figure, then she turned back to Kiall. 'Remind me to have a word with you. In the morning.'

'I'm ready to have a word. Now.'

'With me in my nightie?'

'I've seen you in a lot less.'

'You have?' She opened her golden eyes wide. 'Oh, that—that was years ago. Everything we talk about seems to end up in the same way. It's all rooted in your subconscious. You like to see me as a scarlet woman. To use an obscene term, a harlot. Now that I think of it, how dare you?'

'I'm well aware, Alison, you use aggression as your first line of defence, but it won't work. What did you say to Karen that reduced her to such a mess?'

'Maybe I told her it was about time she started demanding

a ring.'

He looked at her very searingly, his extraordinary eyes glittering. 'You have the gall to bring *me* into this?'

'You have the gall to deny you've been leading her a merry dance?' Ally threw her head up, looking very spirited and mettlesome.

'Tell me about it.' His voice was filled with a taunting *diablerie*. 'You seem to have been doing a lot of enquiring into my background.'

'Not at all.' She stood her ground, folding her elegant arms and sliding them into her lace-trimmed satin sleeves. 'Karen Fulbrook is your business. I only wish it would stay that way.'

'You invite trouble,' he said with a flicker of malice.

'I like that!'

'I've never met a woman so challenging and direct.'

'And you don't like it, do you? No doubt about it. You've got a little problem there.'

'And you've got a big one if you won't admit at least one man as your master. Men do rule the earth, Alison. And you know why? It's their role. It's what nature equipped them for. Woman is supposed to be the loving companion, the wife and the mother. God knows, that should be demanding enough.'

'Certainly, only men are intoxicated with power. They completely forget women are people as well as companions. You've been trying to repress me from the moment we met.'

'Bless you!' He laughed outright. 'I don't find too much aggression and intelligence convenient in my lady friends.'

'Because you've gone a lifetime without being challenged?'

'Maybe, but there's something very unpleasant about being branded an exploiter and manipulator of women. Don't think for one moment I'm going to put up with your contempt.'

'Then let me chase you out. This is my bedroom.' A current of hostility and excitement was flowing between them, making her nervous behind her cloak of defiance.

'So we'll change territory,' he suggested darkly. 'Come to mine.'

Colour flared under Ally's creamy skin. 'I promise you, I'll never do that.'

'I can't break you down?' Naked sensuality sprang into his eyes.

'Wait for the next house-guest.' Immediately she said it, Ally knew she had gone too far. She could see by his arrested posture that the barb had gone home. He uncoiled like a dangerous animal, stalking slowly and single-mindedly towards her. The overhead chandelier struck blue lights in his coal-black hair, glanced off his high cheekbones, the purposeful set of his mouth and his jaw. He looked magnificent and menacing, his eyes impaling her with their sword-like glitter.

'If you're planning to beat me,' she cried sharply, 'it won't do.'

He laughed quietly, not a flash of humour in his eyes.

'Karen's not the only one who can scream. For your information, I took voice-production lessons.'

'Then let it roll.'

'Kiall . . .'

'Oh, I just *love* it when you turn into a mere mortal. Just when it suits you.'

'It's all the defence I've got.'

'You're so right!' He grasped her with soft savagery, hauling her to him and smothering her uplifted, open mouth with his own.

She resisted wildly, breathlessly, because he was crushing her, but no sound escaped their locked mouths. A furious excitement spiralled through Ally, so that, even as she fought him, deep within her was that aching to have him capture and devastate all her defences. Everything about him was so frighteningly, perfectly acceptable to her: his clean male taste and scent, the faint rasp of his polished skin, the irresistible magnetism of his strong, lean body. She loved the way his hair grew from the striking widow's peak to the thick, longish hair at the base of his fine neck. She loved the warm strength of the lean, long-fingered hands that covered hers. His attraction for her was unearthly. She was beginning to believe it was ordained.

'What is it?' He drew back sharply, staring down into her exquisitely aroused face. 'Tell me.'

She sighed deeply and her voice drifted into a soft, husky murmur. 'I cannot.'

'Because you don't like what happens to you?'

'I like it so much, it frightens me.'

'And you believe I want another woman?'

'I believe two are too many.'

'Witch! You've made this place magic.'

She wanted to lift her arms and pull his beautiful dark head to her breast. This feeling, this love, was too powerful for her. She wasn't ready for it yet. There had to be commitment to go with the wild passion.

'Do you want to tell me about tonight?'

She put the tips of her fingers across his mouth. 'How much interest could you possibly have in girl-talk? Karen simply thought she'd get her money's worth.'

'That scream sounded dreadfully familiar,' he admitted. 'I've heard it before.'

'Her whole existence centres around you,' Ally offered gravely.

'There aren't all that many men in the big league.' He shrugged. 'I assure you, if I lost everything tomorrow, you wouldn't see her for dust.'

'Cross your fingers you don't.'

'And what about you, Ally? What would your reactions be if I lost Mowana?'

'Please, don't even think about it. It scares me. I know what

Mowana means to you.'

'But you're involved,' he insisted, his handsome face filled with a hard light. 'I'm asking you a hypothetical question.'

'I guess I'd agonise for you,' Ally said truthfully.

'But look for someone else to snap up?'

She sighed at his cynicism, thinking the woman he finally settled on wouldn't have an easy time. 'If that's what you think. This is where you fall apart, Kiall. Magnificent as you are, your feelings are all jammed up about women.'

He laughed shortly. 'Most women look for a good provider.'

'That makes sense,' she agreed. 'Most women want children, and one has to be able to care for them. Marriage means responsibility, and that colours most women's view of a mate.'

'You want children?'

'Certainly I do!' Her large eyes sparkled. 'I love children. I don't want to miss out on the precious relationship a mother has with her child. The feeling must be incomparable.'

There was something disturbing in the twist of his mouth. 'Not all women see motherhood in that way.'

'I know.' She forced herself to move away from him, the very image of a highly desirable woman. 'But there are so many destructive forces in life. Marriage is so close, the stresses could be great. You never mention if you ever see your mother . . .'

His diamond eyes glittered brilliantly. 'You don't think I should deal as harshly with her as she did with me?'

Ally found herself gently wringing her hands. 'Have you never thought it must have nearly killed her to say goodbye to you?'

'No, Ally, I haven't,' he returned bitingly. 'You're presuming an attachment that wasn't there. Don't wring your heart for me, lady. I don't need it. Women ditch their children every day. I can tell you one thing, God help the woman who tries to get away from me.'

At breakfast next morning there were dark, bruised smudges beneath Karen's eyes, but her manner was brisk and as brittle as usual. 'I think we should start on the guest-list for the polo match, don't you?' she said crisply.

'I hardly think we need organising, Karen,' Sacha protested, fairly mildly.

'I wonder.' Karen gave one of her narrow smiles and Ally, who had been feeling sorry for her, now didn't know why. Karen really was a bitch, and she never let either Susan or Sacha forget for a minute that she considered their manner and behaviour was uncharacteristic of the landed gentry. 'I suggest we have——' She reeled off at least twenty names. 'That's besides the families of the players, of course.'

'I loathe Caroline Pierce,' Sacha said quickly, looking dismayed. 'I really don't want her here.'

'Then why have her?' Ally questioned, having never learnt to keep her mouth shut.

'Do you mind?' Karen turned her sleek head and gave Ally a flat stare. 'Caroline Pierce is the widow of one of our biggest property-owners. Kiall would be certain to want her here. Of course, being an outsider, you wouldn't know that.'

'That woman is terribly rude to Mum,' Sacha said desperately.

'Not really, darling,' Karen mocked. 'You just don't appreciate her style.'

'So much for style! What's wrong with good manners?' Ally said challengingly. 'I wouldn't tolerate anyone being rude to me in my own home.'

'Kiall's home, don't you mean?'

'So?' Sacha cried angrily. 'We've been living here all our lives.'

'And you're Kiall's family,' Ally added grimly. 'Honestly,

Karen, the things you say. I haven't the slightest doubt Kiall would be very angry if you ever dared repeat them in front of him.'

'Are you trying to threaten me?' Karen asked in icy tones.

'There doesn't seem to be any other way. Susan and Sacha are too nice to tell you to pull your head in. But I don't have any trouble at all.'

'You're common, that's why.' Karen's eyes snapped disdainfully.

'I'd say Ally was a true lady,' Susan interrupted, with such severity that Karen looked as if an old family pet had suddenly jumped up and bitten her. 'I really do think you should get yourself in hand, Karen. You're becoming very hard and bitter.'

'What?' Karen's golden skin flushed scarlet, and she drew back visibly in her chair.

'If you want me to repeat it, I will. Until Ally came here I'd got into the way of ignoring your unkind little remarks, but I see now that was weak, an opting out of asserting myself as I should. I've sacrificed a great deal for a quiet life. Now, in middle age, I wonder why. I will not endure any more, Karen. Until Kiall marries, I am the mistress of Mowana. And I will put together the guest-list. I'll even invite Caroline Pierce. I know she'll make a point of trying to put me down, but this time she might be in for a surprise.'

'Why, Susan!' Karen tried to revive herself with a gulp of strong coffee. 'I can't believe you felt this way. I've always loved coming here. I thought you were my friend, but now it seems Miss Allen has turned you against me.'

'I'll admit she has made me see things more clearly,' Susan answered with quiet composure. 'My courage, self-confidence, had almost disappeared. Always so apologetic, *poor Susan.* I've decided to try to put my life in order. Perhaps take control.'

'Attagirl, Mum!' Sacha looked startled and happy.

'I'm not a very articulate woman,' Susan continued. 'I'm not, like Ally, able to defend myself with a quick wit. Most often when people hurt me I want to burst into tears, and I have not been spared by you and women like you, Karen. You wear two faces. The mask of friendship when Kiall is around, and when he isn't you try very hard to let me know you don't consider me one of the élite class. I know your mother is responsible, a great deal, for your attitude. She regards herself as very nearly perfect. Some might see her as an appalling snob.'

'Please leave my mother out of this,' Karen exclaimed tightly, starting to fold her napkin.

'With pleasure.' Susan's soft, pretty face had overnight gained definition. 'I have no objection to your inviting your entire family here, Karen, for the polo match and the party after. I assume your brother will be playing, in any case. What I am saying is this: I'll expect you all to conduct yourselves differently. I always had a terrible fear when you were all about. I know you enjoyed ganging up on me. Cruel, really, when you think about it. Ally, more than anyone, has made me see the stupidity of my suffering. *I* am responsible for *me*. Perhaps in my forties I'll come of age.'

'Your friend has done this, you know,' Karen shrieked at Sacha, and leapt to her small feet.

'Oh, sure!' Sacha responded, looking up at her.

'I'd like to be able to tell you what I really think of her,' Karen choked.

'Opportunist, wasn't it?' Ally met Karen's furious eyes.

'I can promise you I'll prove it,' Karen said, and her voice shook.

'How? Steal the silver and stash it away in my room?'

'It's the sort of thing you might do,' Karen sneered, holding her side as though she were racked with pain.

'You'll be wanting to leave some time today, Karen, won't

you?' Susan interrupted. 'I know you always have a beautiful new dress for a party, and it will give you time to fly off to Brisbane or Sydney and have a good look around.'

'I'll be speaking to Kiall about that!' Karen angled her pointed chin, so shocked that she appeared to have shrunk.

'Maybe I'll have a word with him myself,' Susan responded wryly. 'He works so hard, I've always tried to keep unpleasantness from him.'

'I really don't know when I've been so upset.' Karen shook her head vehemently. 'We've had hundreds of visitors out here, hundreds, but this is the first time anyone has tried to undermine our friendship. You'll pay for it, Miss Allen, you'll see!' She flounced out, her small riding-boots clattering over the polished floors.

'Thank God we got that over before the men returned,' Susan murmured. 'I feel terribly shaky inside.'

'I think you did blessedly well.' Ally reached over and patted Susan's hand, perturbed to find it was indeed trembling.

'I wonder what she'll tell Kiall,' Sacha said, round-eyed.

'Kiall has her measure,' Ally stated admantly. 'Now, speaking of new dresses, why don't we all get one?'

'Why not?' Susan smiled, making an enormous effort to throw off the upset that was trying to flood her system. Little did anyone know what even that episode had taken out of her.

'I know exactly where to buy the best clothes all over the country,' Ally said quickly, her sharp young eyes more observant of Susan than Susan imagined. 'I'm going to make you gorgeous, Mrs Lancaster.'

'Ally, dear, you're wasting your time,' Susan protested.

'Believe it.' Ally leaned forward, willing Susan's confidence to hold. 'You're very youthful-looking, and you've kept your figure. I would suggest restyling your hair.' Her gaze roamed over Susan, very clear and professional. 'I promise you, Susan, with only a little application you'll really enjoy your new image.'

'Mum will never allow it,' Sacha said. 'Don't think I haven't tried to get her out of the groove.'

'What do you say, Susan?' Ally placed her hand on Susan's wrist.

'I'd like to impress my detractors.'

'Then impress them you will!' Ally cried happily. 'It will be a piece of cake. I m getting all excited just thinking about it.'

'It's about time I bothered,' Susan said in a girlish voice. 'I might even put myself on a little diet. I'll speak to Mrs Tanner, for that matter. I don't know what you said to her, Ally, but she's so much more approachable.'

'Because she doesn't feel isolated,' Ally smiled. 'Kiall promised her a trip in the Beech Baron. Could be he might take us all to Brisbane. I know an excellent designer there.'

'Forgive me,' Sacha gave a wail, 'but when are you going to speak to him about Leon? I'll go crazy if I don't see him.'

'Some time this morning.' Ally's confident smile concealed her trepidation. 'It wasn't the right time, floundering in the mud.'

Ally was dressed for riding when she saw Major Dawson return to the house. He came up on to the veranda where Susan was standing looking out, and Ally saw him take Susan's hand and carry it to his lips in a most gallant fashion. His expression was full of joy in the morning, and his voice rumbled with warmth and good humour. Ally held back until he had walked into the house and headed towards the guest wing, then she made her own way out on to the veranda.

'Such a nice man!' She came up behind Susan, murmuring with deep meaning.

'The nicest.' Susan looked very pink and self-conscious.

'I would say he has a definite *tendresse* for you,' Ally said softly.

'No, Ally!' Susan looked shocked and surprised.

'Yes, Susan,' Ally teased. 'Anyone could tell you, even if they wore blinkers. Surely you realise he pays you a good deal of attention?'

Susan stared at Ally almost blankly for a full five seconds. 'He's just such a gentleman,' she shrugged off.

'OK, I admit that,' Ally agreed smoothly, 'but he likes to make little excuses to touch you.'

'It's not true, Ally,' Susan protested, starting to hug herself.

'Would you like it to be true?' Ally asked in her direct style.

'Oh, Ally!' Susan looked down, biting her tender lip.

'Why do you think it so strange a man might be interested in you?' Ally demanded. 'You're a very attractive woman by anyone's standards.'

'*Au naturel?*' Susan looked up and laughed.

'All the better. You look good with or without make-up, and Major Dawson knows it. I would say you conform to all that he wants in a woman. You're genuinely sweet and totally without malice. You're intelligent and, importantly, you have spiritual values. You're very well read, though unlike me you try to hide your light beneath a bushel. Major Dawson finds you delightful, and he's the kind of man on whom a woman can depend.'

'Sturdy as an oak.' Susan nodded. 'I've never thought of remarrying, Ally. Never. Sacha wouldn't like it.'

'Sacha!' Ally clicked her tongue. 'Sacha has become used to her mum's sacrifices. You're a young woman, Susan. There are lots of years yet. Sacha will be off and married. You know that. I know it; whether or not it's Leon Keppler is another thing. You have a right to happiness. Why keep clipping your wings?'

Susan consulted the lifeline on her open palm. 'And that's your opinion, Ally?' Her blue eyes were softly dazzling.

'Use your own senses,' Ally told her gently. 'Nothing's

wrong with them. You know Major Dawson is attracted to you.'

Susan sighed deeply. 'I have thought about it,' she admitted.

'Give him half a chance and he'll sweep you off your feet.' Ally only half joked. She thought it could happen.

Susan shook her fair head. 'Kiall woud think I was mad,' she exclaimed in dismay.

'Naturally,' Ally grinned. 'Kiall thinks anyone would be mad to get married. That's his problem, not yours.'

'Oh, Ally, Ally,' Susan whispered. 'Nothing is easy.'

'It's easier if we make a start.'

'How did you learn so much for your age?' Susan asked almost shyly.

'I jot a lot down in notebooks.' Ally set her cream, wide-brimmed cattleman's hat on her head, and tilted it to a rakish angle. 'How do I look?'

'Magnificent,' Susan said simply. 'Absolutely magnificent.'

'All I need now is my horse!'

CHAPTER SIX

'WHERE you goin', miss?' Billy the young aboriginal hand asked her after he had given her a leg-up on to Yasmin.

'Not far, Billy, don't worry.'

'Have to worry, miss.' The black liquid eyes looked up at her, torn between anxiety and merriment. 'Probably the Boss would kill me if you been and got lost.'

'No need to rub it in.'

'People get lost.' Billy grinned. 'Even bright ones like you.'

'I won't get lost today, Billy,' Ally said reassuringly. 'Just point me in the right direction.'

'Pink Lady Lagoon.' Billy pointed a skinny arm to an area within a relatively short distance. 'Sure about this, miss?' Billy protested.

Ally nodded. 'I told Mr Kiall I'd be riding out this morning.'

Billy drew level with Yasmin's head, staring into one big, luminous eye and murmuring to the Arab in a soft tribal dialect, 'You look after her, hear?'

'Oh, she will. I attach all my safety to this darling creature.' Ally leaned forwards to pat Yasmin's elegantly arched neck. 'The lagoon isn't far, anyway. I'm really looking forward to this ride.'

It was a beautiful morning and a beautiful scene. Ally rode through the open grassland, her mood very carefree. She didn't intend that the morning's scene with Karen should cloud that perfect day. The sky was the deep, flawless blue of an opal, not one cloud in it, the sun pure gold. Her cream slouch hat protected her face from the worst of its brilliant rays, just as her yellow silk scarf, lightly knotted around her throat, protected the vulnerable nape. She had taken to plaiting her long hair for her ride, and the style was practical and wonderfully cool.

'Come on, Yasmin,' she said. 'Let's try a little gallop just as far as that tree.'

It was like floating. Ally couldn't get over how much pleasure she derived from riding. It even seemed to her that the little Arab shared her sense of *joie de vivre*. She was the most wonderful companion and Ally knew she would miss all this terribly when it was time for her to leave.

The birds, as usual, accompanied her, a mantle of brilliant colour, and she wished she could ride to the Garanda Hills in the shimmering distance, where there were marvellous aboriginal rock paintings glowing miraculously against grey rock. There were galleries all over the vast station, including a number of sacred sites. There was even a cave full of drawings of the first white man who had come to Mowana a long time ago. Charles Lancaster riding a giant horse. Kiall had promised to take her on a tour, but it woud take the whole day. As it was, she couldn't fit everything in. Sacha preferred lazing around the pool at the homestead, but Ally, the 'doer', treasured the opportunity to explore the blossoming Mother Earth. During her stay, at least, it was wondrously lush, so that riding through miles of wild flowers was a vivid experience.

Pink Lady Lagoon was a wonderful moon-shaped stretch of water, one of the numerous lagoons and billabongs that criss-crossed the huge property. Ally could see it shining through the lacy fretwork of the trees. Cattle had been brought in from many miles away and confined in special holding yards while the vet took a look at them. Ally could hear the lowing like a constant dull roar. She thought she could do with a cup of billy tea, even if she had to swallow it in Karen's presence. Karen followed Kiall round with a fanatical determination. Maybe simple determination was the way to whittle his resistance down.

'He's mine, and I won't let you have him!' Ally remembered the other girl's warming, spoken in anguish.

Karen was the most vehement, potentially most dangerous woman she had ever known. It was true she wore masks. Look how loyal, how supportive she was with Kiall, while denying his womenfolk any respect at all. Ally felt proud of Susan's stand this morning. It had taken a lot for Susan to speak out. The role of inadequacy as wife and chatelaine of a great station had been thrust upon her. She had been very young when Austin Lancaster had chosen her, no doubt deliberately to ensure his mastery, and she had used passivity as a defence mechanism to help cope with her difficult life. Susan had privately confided to Ally that she had 'never felt important to anyone,' including her own daughter. Such an attitude didn't go with self-esteem, but Ally could quite see how it had all happened. Susan had been powerless for most of her life, now she was breaking free from her chains.

Ally had timed her arrival nicely, for the men were stopping for a tea-break, provided by a diminutive Chinese called Ho. Karen, the only female member of the group, looked around in astonishment as Ally rode in. Kiall, in conversation with the vet, wheeled just as suddenly, the frown that was gathering easing into an expression of wry admiration.

'Have you never heard of walk before you gallop?' he challenged as he joined her.

'Yasmin loves to gallop,' she told him, dismounting in very creditable style. 'I'd dearly love a cup of tea.'

'Think you're a real jillaroo, don't you?' He took the reins from her and passed them to his foreman.

'I think I could be happy.' She took off her slouch hat and ran her fingers through the silky hair that grew back from her temples.

'At least you look the part,' he said critically.

'I am the part,' she told him with a bright, eager expression. 'I just love riding.'

'Just see you keep to short distances,' he admonished her. 'You're no Princess Anne yet.'

The men greeted her with the gentle courtesy she had come to know, then went back to their conversations. Karen, surprisingly, brought her a mug of tea, but as she went to pass it down to Ally, who was seated comfortably with her back against a tree, she tripped over a tree root and the scalding liquid splashed out over Ally's shirt, then ran down into the coarser material of her jeans.

'Oooh!' Ally drew a shallow, shuddering breath as the hot tea quickly soaked the thin cotton of her shirt, the light bra beneath, and thence burned her creamy skin.

'Get up.' Never a man to waste a second, Kiall hauled her to her feet and rushed her down to the lagoon. He freed the red kerchief he wore at his neck and bent to soak it in the water. Then he straightened and drenched Ally's shirt.

It was cold. Blissfully cold, soothing the area of smarting.

'You can soak me if you hurry.' She felt quite giddy for a moment, but still she joked.

'You really should take that damned blouse off.' He kept his hand on her wrist and his eyes had darkened to a gathering storm.

'It's all right.'

'Are you sure?' he asked very sombrely. 'That must have been scalding.'

'I know you'd like to look, but you must take my word.'

'You've gone white.' His tone was filled with concern, and something dark and alien.

'It happened so suddenly.'

'This time, Karen has overstepped the mark.' His tone was harsh.

'I think she knows that.' Ally lifted her head and her eyes fell on Karen, standing well back with the men. No one, it seemed, dared intrude, though all the men were obviously dismayed by the incident.

'I can offer you my shirt.' Even as he was speaking, his eyes were settling on a sheltered grove of acacias. Quickly, he stripped off his shirt and passed it to her, warm from the heat of his body.

'I don't want this, Kiall.' She felt a rush of emotion that almost made her cry.

He seemed to look at her across a long way. 'I won't have you humiliated. Take it and put it on. The men will turn away.'

The men had already gone about their business with great tact. A sense of foreboding had got through to all of them, for, self-possessed as she was, Karen's clumsy movement had revealed an age-old jealousy.

Ally went behind the thick green screen and stripped off her shirt and her bra. A large area of red flamed on her sensitive skin, but Kiall's quick action had helped a lot. She was more upset by the vindictiveness of Karen's action than the smarting burns. If Karen could act like that as a woman with no rights, what would she be like as a jealous wife? In the area of female venom, Karen could outmatch her any day; indeed, so tolerant was Ally, she felt a queer pity for the older girl. She had a clear picture of Kiall's eyes, combining disgust with an icy anger.

The shirt, pale olive in colour and almost military in

design, was much, much too big for her. She criss-crossed it over her body, tucking it into her jeans and securing it with her wide, silver-buckled belt. She was trembling a little, as though from her exertion. Jealousy was such an ugly emotion, one of the world's evils. Karen had been putting herself through years of internal conflict. She should have handled the situation differently. She should have had a showdown with Kiall, and then if her feelings were not reciprocated she should have started seeking a man who would care for her. By turning all her anger on other women, as though they were somehow to blame, was perpetuating a destructive cycle.

When Ally walked back into the clearing, Karen had already gone, and Kiall's lean, muscular torso was sheathed in a black T-shirt that his foreman had rustled up from his saddlebag.

'Nothing to worry about,' Ally reported with a lightness she didn't feel. 'My skin's a bit red, but it will fade.' Her huge, gold-starred eyes looked beyond him. 'Karen gone back to the homestead?'

'I never felt less like talking about Karen,' Kiall said bluntly. 'She acts like an adolescent who can't control her feelings.'

'It could have been an accident,' Ally said despairingly.

'Next time it'll be a stampede, and she'll let the cattle trample right over you.'

'So whose fault is it, this obsession?'

'Who can explain women?' Kiall returned harshly. 'They're always a threat to someone. Especially when they're hitting thirty.'

'That's preposterous!'

'Is it?' He looked as arrogant as the devil.

'Are you saying women regard the age of thirty as some

tremendous milestone?' Ally demanded.

'It all has to do with catching a husband.'

'I protest.'

'Well, you're not going to protest around here. I'm the boss.' He got a firm hold on her arm and led her towards a parked jeep.

'So what am I going to do?' She looked up at him in surprise. 'There's no limit to your high-handedness. My feet are barely touching the ground.'

'You must adore it,' he returned sarcastically. 'Beautiful as you are, most men would have to worship at your feet. As befitting a goddess. Come along, Alison. My men are going to great lengths to ignore us, but just how long do you think that's going to last? Get in the jeep. You can't go back to the house until Karen's gone, so I'll take you out to Garanda.'

A few moments longer, while Kiall gave his foreman instructions, and they were heading out towards the Garanda Hills and a paradise of the wild. The billabongs after the rain were teeming with bird-life, spectacular to watch. Ally turned her head to watch a tall jabiru fishing the shores of a lagoon, its long red legs in vivid contrast to its black and white plumage. Smaller grey and white elegant birds picked their way across the blue lotus pads which were like floating steps in a stream. She had never seen so many birds. It was amazing and, what was most beautiful of all, Mowana was always ringing with birdsong from the moment she opened her eyes to the very last of the light.

'How many millions of birds are there out here?' she asked dreamily, as a flock of gaudy parrots burst out of a beautiful old gum.

'Well, Australia is known as the Land of Parrots, and Queensland can easily claim some of the most beautiful and unique flora and fauna in the world. Can you imagine

what it all must have looked like to Charles Lancaster when
he first arrived here? After all, we're in the tropics, a far cry
from England, and even now we're not far from the jungle,
and the wildlife is prolific. You can see some of our lagoons
are miles long. The Blue Lady is at least three miles long,
and it supports about a hundred thousand water birds, I
would say. You're here at the best time. It takes the coming
of the Wet to set Mowana on fire. My grandmother planted
all the magnificent jacarandas and poincianas, the tulip
trees, the bauhinias and cascaras, so everywhere you look
there are great bursts of colour against the dense green. I've
been in most places of the world, but to my mind it's very
hard to beat the top end of our continent—the tropical
richness, the vast plains, the endless miles of spectacular
beaches and the ultimate beauty of the Great Barrier Reef.
Even born here, I'm always awed by our little pocket of
civilisation every time I fly in. I think one has to fly to
appreciate the magnitude of the country. Queensland is an
immense state. And, of course, it's largely unpopulated.
Further north again, Cape York Peninsula is still a kind of
no-man's-land. Very few get past Cooktown.'

'Have you?'

'I've stood on the very top of Cape York, looking out at
Torres Strait. I was seventeen years old and my father was
beside me. We had a great friend as well. A man called
Marty Thormann, an American who bought up a dozen
run-down stations, brought in Brahman cross-breeding and
showed the rest how to do it. Marty was a great man.'

'What happened to him?'

'Believe it or not, he was shot by a cattle duffer.
Accidentally, it was claimed. Marty was nearly eighty and
one tough old guy. The police had a job stopping the locals
from organising a lynching party. Marty was what this
country is all about. He might have been born in the

States, but most people will remember him as a great Australian.'

Ally was quiet for a moment. 'You wouldn't want to be anything else but a cattleman?' she mused.

He shrugged. 'It's a huge job. I regard our beef as the best in the world. Queensland is the home of the cattle kings, you know. Horses and cattle, that's my world.'

'Plus a wild kingdom. That might be the greatest resource of all. Vast tracts of natural landscape must be rare.'

'As are the rock paintings I'm going to show you. They're quite startlingly fresh, yet some of them have been there for thousands of years. In the early days, the local tribes must have used Mowana as ceremonial grounds. There are vast galleries of rock paintings in Australia, but the finest and most elegant are the "Mimi" figures of Arnhem Land. They were believed to be skilled spirit hunters who lived in the area before man and taught the aborigines how to hunt. The large friezes of running, dancing, hunting figures are extraordinary, and they're right across the escarpment. Some of the figures wear the most fantastic head-dresses, and in some they hunt the Tasmanian tiger that became extinct on the mainland about eleven thousand years ago. In fact, archaeologists date many of the paintings to about twenty thousand years. I find aboriginal art fascinating, and of course it's a very beautiful and tangible record of their occupation of this continent over the past thirty thousand years. Our own paintings are far from insignificant. We've had many archaeologists out here from time to time, and we're all very protective of what we've got. I would like to think my great-great-great-grandsons could look on what I'm going to show you today, just as Charles Lancaster recorded his first sightings in his journal. So that you won't be taken unawares, I should tell you a lot of the paintings are of birds and animals and strange spirit figures, but others are of humans in all scenes of life, including plenty of making love, both sacred and profane.'

They left the jeep at the base of the rugged, low-lying Garandas, which were framed in a peculiar dancing blue light.

'What is it?' Ally asked, shading her eyes with her hand and staring upwards.

'I don't know, but it's always been like that,' he explained casually. 'A quicksilver heat haze. Old Charlie calls it a fire dance of the all-powerful spirits!'

'It's unbelievable.'

'Most people find it amazing,' he agreed. 'It could be a blue haze off the eucalypts, like the haze over the Blue Mountains. All I know is that it has always framed the Garandas.'

'It's so quiet,' Ally almost whispered as the thought struck her. 'Where are the birds?'

He pointed behind him. 'They're all gathered in the trees, but for some reason they sit silently looking towards the hills. Apparently, it's not all that unusual at sacred cave sites. Don't forget, the Great Spirits made the birds and all creatures. They gather but they don't whistle or shriek or sing. Perhaps the area is mystical. Perhaps the birds are singing but we can't hear them. We might be sealed off in another world.'

'It certainly feels like it.' Ally began to rub the goose-flesh on her arms.

'We'll start there.' Kiall pointed to the visible rock shelters to the north-east. 'Some of the sites are too rugged to get to, and some are guarded by snakes. So many, you can't count them.'

'Gosh!' Despite herself, Ally swallowed nervously.

'Don't worry. I won't let anything hurt you. We'll follow

the path and I'll go ahead to ensure everything is OK. I try
to keep the spirit path cleared, but one shower of rain can
turn the place back to jungle.'

'Oh no, not again.' Ally shuddered, rushed forwards and
grasped him around the waist.

'What is it?' He reacted swiftly.

'Another enormous lizard.' Her cry seemed to echo in
this quiet place.

'He won't hurt you,' Kiall replied. 'He's all curled up,
taking a snooze. The story goes that our great deposits of
red iron oxide were formed by the blood of the giant lizards.
He won't bother you unless you challenge him.'

'And I'm not about to do that.'

'You can keep your arms around my waist if you like. Just
between the two of us, I didn't think you had a timid bone
in your body.'

'Most people would respect six-foot iguanas.'

'Goannas,' he corrected.

'It looks like a crocodile.'

'We used to have crocs around here. There are paintings
of crocodiles in the caves. If you think that's a monster, you
should see the East Indian Komodo dragon. Our giant
monitors can get to about seven feet, but theirs reach nine
or ten.'

'What does it eat?'

'Not people. It's been known to run at horsemen. I once
saw someone mistake a crocodile for a log. The guy nearly
died of fright. The Japanese love our frilled lizard.
Magnified on the screen, it looks the most exotic of
prehistoric monsters. Here, keep your hand tucked in my
belt. We walk. We don't run. We act respectful. We don't
want to make the gods angry.'

'It's getting so I'd be happy to go back to the jeep.

'Do you want to?' He swung on her, his silver eyes

searching.

'No, no. I love it. You know me and my little jokes.

'I'm learning.'

Small round fruit hung in golden globules, startlingly bright against the living green. There were so many of them, it looked almost like a plantation. For the most part, Ally kept her eyes down, following the ochre-red track. Strange patterns lay across the naked earth. Animal tracks? What animals? There was no doubt in her mind that this was a strange place. Shadowy, purple, magenta-fringed lilies, standing little more than six inches high, formed a striking ground cover, interspersed with smouldering blue flowers the shape and size of pansies. Still there was no noise, yet a great mass of wildfowl passed overhead. It just got quieter and quieter.

Perspiration gathered around the brim of her slouch hat, trickled down the channel between her breasts. She flickered a downward glance at her skin. The red had faded to pink. As they climbed higher, there were lizards everywhere. Not the remarkable great goannas, but the smaller variety, sunning themselves on rocks. Once, the great lizards swam in the sea, and even today Mowana's huge goannas crossed the lagoons. They weren't nearly so lovable as the gentle-faced kangaroos, Ally thought.

Nearing the caves the earth emanated a pungent and powerful fragrance, a combination of jasmine and gardenia, with something mysterious besides. Ally looked in all directions, but she could see no flowering tree or vine to suggest where the heavy perfume came from. Clumps of native grasses grew at intervals, and that eerie blue light grew brighter the higher they ascended. Her persistent fantasy was that they were on another planet, with now a small, azure blue bird for a guide. It had appeared suddenly, acting as though it were expected, darting

from rock to rock until they made the entrance to the first
cave. Ally was too astonished to talk. There were so many
things she wanted to draw Kiall's attention to, but her voice
seemed stilled in her throat.

When they entered the cave they both had to stand still
for a few moments, waiting until their eyes had become
accustomed to the transition from brilliant sunlight to a soft
pinky glow. Kiall did not speak but put out a hand, tilting
her chin, and as he did so she saw a great frieze of birds in
the rockwall sky.

One by one the rock shelters welcomed them, the walls
covered with striking images representing the spirit
ancestors. There were engravings of all the animals and
birds, one cave contained the red-ochre painting of a huge
snake that writhed across the wall and the ceiling.
Sometimes the spirit forms suggested European ghosts,
other times space travellers. There were human figures
with spears and boomerangs, abstract symbols that made
powerful artistic statements. The caves and the subject
matter of the paintings varied enormously. Ally saw the
first white man, Charles Lancaster, on his giant horse, and
other paintings where he was followed by stockmen and
cattle, with aboriginal figures hiding in the bushes,
trembling in fear. There were white men with weapons,
and white men apparently dying under the spell of the
mighty Sun Woman. Trees like pandanus stretched across
the walls; drawings that looked like long white clouds,
sorcery figures upside-down. There were even little
creatures that looked like monkeys. Monkeys? Had
Australia been part of southern Asia thousands of years
ago?

It was impossible to witness the pictorial way of life of the
first people to the great continent without falling silent.
One could believe the great spirit ancestors formed the

earth during the Dreamtime, making epic journeys to create
rivers, mountains, and all the great features. Before the
Dreamtime there were no deep lagoons, no hills, no beautiful trees and grasses, no fruits of the earth. There were no
birds and animals, no living creatures. The spirit ancestors
fashioned it all and, when they had done that, they handed
down the Law.

When they entered the cave of Love Magic, Ally gave an
involuntary, strangled gasp. There were dozens of graphic
drawings of men and women enjoying or enticing the
desired person. A traditional form of love magic was
drawing a representation of the desired one on a rock
shelter. A man might draw his sexual fantasy so that, with
the spirits' help, the reality might happen during the same
night.

Ally stood back a little distance, as startled as if she had
come on highly erotic paintings in a modern art gallery. In
fact, the atmosphere of eroticism was so strong that she
could feel herself flushing. No love-magic rite had not been
drawn, including sorcery. Cult totems lined the walls.
Women with round breasts and long nipples were being
either enraptured, ravished or threatened. Some of the
women had obviously been unfaithful, because weapons
circled their heads. The images, ancient as they were in
white and black, yellow and red ochre, were very, very
powerful. Desire and jealousy pulsed from the walls.

'Let's go,' Ally whispered, tugging on Kiall's hand. Her
golden-amber eyes were wide with a kind of superstitious
awe, and the pink glow threw a lovely colour over her face.

'Who's a witch now?' His jewelled glance slid over her, so
light, yet with extraordinary depth, like a bottomless lake.

'This is pretty potent stuff.' The atmosphere of the cave
was pressing on her.

'And you've got a bad attack of nerves.'

She exhaled a shaky breath. 'I don't want any sorcerer to catch me.'

'Not a spirit one, anyway. You've placed yourself in my power.'

She watched the amusement on his face change to an intense sensuality, and an answering excitement rocketed through her blood.

'Don't you realise just how desirable you are?' he asked, with a suggestion of bright, male hostility.

'There's something about this cave. I don't seem able to move.'

'So I've noticed!' His reaction seemed purely instinctive. He reached for her, everything he did so definite, compelling, reaching . . . taking hold. 'You'll be the first white woman to be made love to in this spot.'

'And what happens if I don't play along?' She tried desperately to beat back his tremendous attraction. She couldn't let it overcome her. 'Not one of those exciting little blows on the head?'

Time, even space, tightened around them. His eyes gleamed, their impact so powerful that she felt it wash over her. 'I have agony of a different sort in mind. You like to act as though you don't care a damn, but what's between us is dangerous business.'

'You mean irrevocably physical!' she pointed out bluntly.

'It's much more than that!' His dark face registered his scorn. 'You're much more to me than a lovely face, fine bones and silky hair. You're very bright and independent, full of spirit, yet you make me feel protective as well. It's not very difficult to feel the hunger in your body.'

'It happens, I'll admit, when you touch me.' Emotion enveloped her.

'I put up a fierce struggle not to.'

'Do you?' She was shocked that he admitted it.

'Many is the night I've wanted to come to your room.'

'You don't think I'd put up much resistance?' Ally's voice was husky, ragged with emotion. She couldn't withstand this tremendous emotional bombardment.

'God, Ally,' he bit out. 'You put up so much resistance, you're wearing yourself out. It's difficult, isn't it, being forced to confront your emotional needs?'

A turbulent current was running between them, giving her that frightening sensation of sliding into dangerous waters. She was trapped again between her warring impulses. What was all her talk anyway, but a smoke-screen developed to hide the depth of her feeling? Yet she challenged him.

'You know why?' she asked brightly. 'You're over-powering. You have this stupendous aura and you use it deliberately. You're a knock-'em-dead man. You do. You want to. Perhaps it's even a kind of revenge against women. There's Karen, so consumed with jealousy she's an incipient hysteric. She's even got *you* worried. I'm way ahead of her in that respect. I'm not going to allow you to capture me. And that's what it's all about, isn't it? War. The war between the sexes, as ancient as this cave. I value my freedom, Kiall Lancaster. You've no idea just how much I value my freedom.'

His arms rose in an involuntary motion, gripping her powerfully, holding her to him. 'It must be demoralising to find your body electric.'

'Because it's touching yours!' There was a terrible tension in her throat. 'I marvel at the way the blood is thumping through my veins. I'm even terrified of this supercharge, but I'm not going to allow my feelings to get the better of me. I refuse to become another of your go-nowhere romances.'

'I wondered when you were going to start hinting at

marriage,' challenged Kiall, mockingly bitter.

She gave a furious gasp, and tried unsuccessfully to break free. 'You believe every woman is after you. As it happens, I'm the odd one who isn't.'

'No matter. You're shaking in my arms. That's the big consolation.'

'I detest men who use their physical strength. It's an abuse of power!' She threw back her head and arched her creamy neck, straining away from him, but the effect was one of incredible sensuality, which was not what she consciously intended.

'Damn you!' said Kiall in a furious burst. 'Damn you.' His anger, passion, ignited from hers flames of excitement that consumed them in fiery sheets. Ally's blood was laced with heat. The painted walls of the cave seemed to tilt crazily. She thought she cried out, but her voice was barely above a whisper.

He crushed her mouth under his own. Crushed it. Vanquished it, his hunger and anger driving him into a kind of delirium. Ally herself didn't care what happened. She was lost in the burning flames, her pleasure so intense she could not stop him. What he demanded, she gave. She was only woman, a perfect instrument for sensation.

The folds of his shirt fell away from her body, revealing her high breasts, the magnetic, blossoming nipples, the shadowy descent to her narrow waist.

There was a faint sheen of sweat on Kiall's sun-coppered skin as he made a visible effort at will-power. His eyes moved down over her beautiful body, and he gave a vaguely tortured gasp. There was a split second when Ally could have stopped him, but she couldn't control the raging in her blood. It was cruel, *cruel,* the force of human passion, a dangerous wilderness . . . the jungle.

His hands closed over her yearning breasts, and still

she thought she cried out that he mustn't do that, but she never spoke at all. She murmured incoherently, her soft little mews turning him almost savage. Her defences were shattered. The safe haven she had built for herself was gone for ever. A strong sense of independence had motivated her life, only to be repudiated by her desperation for this man. She had avoided all risk, now she was inviting the most gigantic risk of all. She had no protection. For her heart or her body. She was trapped by her woman's nature, the physical perfection of her own body turned against her. All strength, all resistance drained out of her under this all-conquering stimulation.

'You're so beautiful,' he muttered violently. 'So beautiful you're sending me out of my mind.'

He didn't stop there, his dark face quite immobile but frighteningly intent. His shirt, the shirt she wore, fell away to the sandy floor, and he turned her across his arms, staring down at her as if he had promised himself this moment for a very long time.

'I want you, Ally,' he said, very low and deliberately, the tension in his face accentuating his finely chiselled features 'You're lucky you've survived so long.'

There was a touch of madness in her, too. 'Survived what?' She stared up into his eyes, her spirit rising even though his silver eyes were appraising every pore of her skin.

'Do you want me to undress you, or are you going to do that yourself?'

And so it was that Ally came back to herself. 'I just might have gone so far, now I'm holding back.'

'Oh?' He caught a gleaming handful of her hair.

'I have not come prepared.' She spoke with great anger, her golden eyes flashing.

'What, no pill?'

'Did you imagine I took it?'

'Wouldn't you need to?'

She struck out at him with extraordinary speed, yet still he caught her wrist. 'It fits, doesn't it? A beautiful woman is always being courted, desired, that kind of thing. A woman like you, with all your lovely airs and graces, could never hide herself.'

'I realise that now I've got my shirt off.' She reached down for it with some relish, shouldering it on. 'Your ideas, Kiall, are too extreme. If you really want to learn, you'll accept that more women value their chastity than those who do not. I've only had one lover in my life. I know that's going to upset you. I truly believed myself in love with him. We were going to be married, but I spotted him in the corner of a restaurant chatting up one of his old girlfriends. I ended our engagement the same day. Sex has to mean something to me. It has to mean a very great deal. I don't actually lead a solitary life. I have lots of male friends. We go about. If I'm really fond of them, I allow them to kiss me. Sometimes I enjoy it, but I don't take them home. I remind myself that my woman's body was designed for a higher order. I'll save it for my husband, and the child at my breast.'

'You're a marvel!' Kiall looked at her more calmly, his handsome face sardonic.

'I think I've been put to the test.' Despite herself, the smart of tears stung her eyes, and she averted her amber head.

'No one else, Alison?' Surprisingly gently, in view of his former dominance, he turned her back to him and he began to button her shirt.

'Do you have to ask me?' She kept her eyes on his lean fingers.

'Maybe you summed me up. My ideas could be too

extreme.'

'Only one lover,' she said.

'I'd better not come across him,' he said bluntly, and raised her chin.

'What would you do, load your gun?'

'I'm as violent as the next man.'

'More violent, don't you mean?'

'I haven't bruised you, have I?'

She had nothing to say to him, and her expression was so soft and vulnerable that he swept her back into his arms. 'The thing is, Ally, I want to be, but I'm not prepared for you. You're not only beautiful and bright, but to me you're original. Probably what you are is the real thing, and that's a lot of woman to take on. Maybe I hate the idea of loving a woman.'

'Maybe *I'm* frightened of the idea of loving *you*.' She looked up at the gallery of rock paintings. 'Love is magic. Spellbinding. It does away with independence.'

He gripped her arms and, as she looked back, full, tender lips parted, he kissed her mouth. 'That's it, isn't it? Becoming another person. Two people being one. A man could find his life shattered if he made the wrong choice.' He released her abruptly and, it seemed to Ally, with great finality.

It wasn't until they were nearing the homestead that Ally was sufficiently in command of herself to broach the subject of Leon Keppler. As it was, her voice faintly trembled.

'You're quite in agreement with a party and so forth for the polo weekend?' She flickered a glance at his strong profile.

'Yes, of course.' He, too, seemed unable to come down to normal.

'I'm looking forward to it.'

'Good.' He didn't smile. 'I'll allow you to present the trophy to the winning team.'

'Surely that right is Susan's or Sacha's?' she suggested quickly.

'They won't mind. I've never seen them so content as when you're around.'

The drone of a plane filled the air and Kiall pulled the jeep off the track, staring upwards into the blue, radiant sky. 'That will be Karen,' he said laconically.

'Poor Karen.'

'After what she did to you? The way she's been?'

'I'm not pitiless. She has an excuse.' Ally bent her head.

'Maybe I'd better put my own house in order,' he said crisply, resting his arm on the wheel, turning sideways and pinning her gaze. 'I'm thirty-four years old. Ten years older than you. A lot of women have been drawn to me.' He shrugged derisively. 'Look what I can give them.'

'That's not it!' The coolness of her tone was equally devastating. 'In my business I meet a lot of handsome men. I meet a lot of men with money and power. Sometimes they combine the lot. Sometimes. What you have is far more compelling than all that. And you know it!'

'I'm a king in an isolated kingdom,' he mocked. 'Women, too, like power. Much as I dislike to say it, there was a time I considered marrying Karen. She's smart, good-looking, she was reared to this way of life, her family were right behind her. I'd been attracted to a dozen women who had crossed my path. Attracted, that's all. There's an almighty chasm between attraction and love. A man could only fail if he tried to jump it. Something in my nature rejects second best. Maybe I'm ruthless, I don't know. I never actually proposed to Karen. We never got around to talking an engagement, but her family sure tried tightening the screws. I didn't like that. Our affair petered out all by itself.'

'Yet she's always around?'

'She wasn't busy at this point of her life.'

'She loves you, Kiall.'

'I wouldn't like to count the number of women who have said they loved me by the end of the day. Women are always desperate to love someone.'

'And why is that so strange?' Ally asked simply. 'To love and be loved is the greatest strength.'

'I'm sorry. Karen wasn't about to collar me. On the other hand, I refuse to run for cover. She was part of my life until she became as venomous as a snake. I'm sure she has worked out she has to find somebody else. I'd give her about two weeks.'

'Do you think she'll come back for the polo match?'

'She might, as her brother Alan will make up my team. I'm sure her mother and father will want to make a day of it. Mowana hospitality used to be legendary. I mean no disrespect to Susan, I'm very fond of her, but she has always been very nervous in company. All our large-scale gatherings came to an end well before my father died. Susan simply couldn't handle them. She gets tremulous when she has to take the reins. You know that. You've only been here a short time and you've reorganised the household.'

'You object?'

'I don't object, Ally,' he said almost wearily. 'I appreciate what you've done.'

'Then could you do something for me?'

He smiled, not a humorous smile, but it showed his beautiful white teeth. 'What's coming next?'

'Would you allow Sacha to invite Leon Keppler for the weekend?' She watched his expression turn as unyielding as steel.

'Give you an inch and you take a mile.'

'All right, don't have him,' Ally said. 'Let Sacha go. Lose her. Is that what you want?'

'What the hell are you talking about?'

'Are you sure you've thought this out carefully? I don't know this Leon Keppler, I've never met him. I do know your feelings, and I don't think Susan is terribly happy about him either. It seems like good psychology to have him and Sacha right under your nose. Sacha is the sort of person who could be driven into something foolish. You issue an order and she simultaneously moves to meet him out of sight. Wouldn't it be better if you and Susan were watching? Susan is anxious about the situation, I know. Sacha isn't exactly an adult yet.'

'That might have something to do with all the babying.'

'Sacha is all Susan has got. She had to have someone to lavish her love on. You didn't need it. I recall you told me your father actively discouraged demonstrations of affection. That leaves us with Sacha herself. She's desperate for affection.'

'She's a damned fool if she's going to make Keppler her hero. Don't make me the villain. I care about my sister. I don't want to see her ruin her young life. I won't see it happen. She has family to look after her.'

'And she has a right to make her own decisions. You can jump in with a little good advice when it will do the most good. Rebellion in the young is common enough. The more you oppose him, make him the victim, the more Sacha makes him a symbol of love and her independence. She feels humiliated when you won't allow her her friends.'

'The problem is, dear Alison,' Kiall gritted his teeth, 'Keppler is not her friend. He can't hide what he is from me. He's a man on the make. He may give the initial impression of education and charm, but he's ruled by a greedy streak. He wants money. Big money. It helps when he can have it with beauty and youth. He expects to rule Sacha's life. He expects to take over the financial reins. Like a fool, she's made it clear to him the trust fund is a very large one.'

'And that's your considered opinion?'

'You want to see him for yourself?'

'I can't think of a better way to arrive at some solution,' Ally said worriedly. 'Sacha doesn't need my opinion. She things she does, of course.'

'The best way to do this to make you an heiress,' Kiall suggested savagely. 'My little sister could never compete with you. Yes, the answer's really simple. We'll pretend you've been left a great fortune by an old admirer. Some feeble-minded old gent with about twenty million in the attic. It will have to be twenty million. Sacha was left ten.'

'Don't you feel guilty with all that money?'

'I'd feel guilty if I didn't make so many contributions to charitable institutions. You want to take control, you managing woman? I urge you to play the role of *femme fatale*. Talk about your money openly. Say you're thinking of buying God knows how many paintings. Mention a few Renoirs and Monets in your harbour-side mansion. Little things that were left to you in an excess of love.'

'Are you serious?' Ally couldn't pretend she wasn't shocked.

'Serious, hell! I'd kill you if you got tangled with a man like Keppler. What I am saying is this: if Keppler is directing his attentions at Sacha now, he'd soon transfer them if a richer, more sophisticated woman turned up. There's no balance between him and Sacha. Sacha is just a kid. Keppler is an old, old shyster, only the grey doesn't show.'

'Sacha has kept his age a secret. Just how old is he?'

'Damn it, he's my age,' Kiall told her with extreme irritation. 'Must you be so literal-minded?'

'Absolutely! I thought I might be witness to some revelation.'

Kiall began drumming his fingers on the wheel. 'I have to think about this, Ally.'

'Naturally, as long as you give me an answer. As of now. The invitations have to go out.'

'The man is a rotter,' Kiall said curtly.

'Then can't we show him up?'

He looked back at her, frowning intently. 'What luxury-loving man wouldn't go after a rich lady?'

'Is this a conundrum?' Ally blinked her golden-amber eyes.

'I'm sure we could find an attractive heiress. No one would pay any attention to your bank balance.'

'How would you know?' Ally tossed up her chin. 'I'll have you know I'll be very well off in maybe four years.'

'Well off!' he muttered, his mouth twisting derisively. 'What you call well off.'

'I still say well off.'

Unexpectedly, his mood lightened and he gave his low, attractive laugh. 'This is between you and me.'

'What is?'

'Wouldn't you say Karen was a reasonably attractive package? Good looks, social position, money.'

'I think she's nuts about someone called Lancaster.'

'I doubt that. I mean, I really doubt that after what I said to her.'

'It must have been awful, the way she took off.'

'Occasionally I get tough.' He leaned forwards and switched on the ignition. 'I assure you, if we dropped a few hints about Karen's suitability, Keppler would disavow my little sister in double-quick time.'

Ally moved uncomfortably, pulling his shirt diagonally across her body. 'Certainly she wouldn't invite me again. I can't do that, Kiall. I don't like meddlers.'

'You do it all the time.' He spun the wheel, and the jeep leapt back on to the track.

CHAPTER SEVEN

WHEN Sacha heard she was free to invite Leon for the polo weekend, she was ecstatic.

'I knew you could do it!' she crowed. 'You've got the patent on managing Kiall.'

Ally held up a palm. 'Believe that, and you'll believe anything.'

'I don't think you give yourself sufficient credit,' Susan smiled. 'What did you say, Ally?'

'I told him I thought he was being a wee bit autocratic,' Ally said with more blitheness than she felt.

'That's because he has always made himself responsible for Sacha's welfare,' Susan said loyally. 'I'm so glad you're going to meet Leon, Ally. We do so want your opinion.'

Sacha snorted. 'Mum thinks I'm an idiot.' She sat on the arm of Ally's chair and hugged her around the shoulders. 'I know you'll find Leon as fascinating as I do. He's so clever and sophisticated. He's very good with women. He really likes them.'

'Why shouldn't he, for God's sake?' Ally asked.

'I've met plenty who don't,' Sacha mused. 'If you can't talk business or politics, the men start walking away. Either they think I'm cute or a bird-brain. Leon is the first man to treat me like a real person, not a dumb girl with nothing to contribute. I know you're going to like him, Ally. I need someone on my side.' And then she was gone, whisking through the door, with a smile and a wave, to write Leon his most important invitation.

'I do hope she won't get hurt,' Susan murmured

uncertainly. 'I have my doubts about Mr Keppler.'

'I've gathered that,' Ally nodded. 'She could be hurt, perhaps, but not destroyed. It seems to me, Sacha's expression of love is more what we work our way through in the teens. Early romantic experiences. A sort of "in love with love" fantasy. Much as she likes to rebel against Kiall's authority, wouldn't you agree it's her safety shield? His authority is her security. I think she's too young for marriage yet, but old enough to be rebelling against control. How does Leon interact with Sacha if he's so much older and more sophisticated?'

'They appear to get on very well,' Susan started. 'I know Kiall believes he's exploiting her youth, but I've been trying very hard to see both sides. He appears to be in love with her, though on a much more restrained scale than Sacha. Her emotions at the moment are a bit unbalanced.'

'They mostly are when one's barely out of school. In a sense, Sacha has led a narrow life. She told me herself she'd had little contact with young men her age. She went to an all-girls' school. She couldn't sustain study, so she missed out on the traditional relationships at university, college and so forth. She has never had to work. In a sense, she's a sitting duck!'

'Trust you to put a name to it, Ally!' From the look on Susan's face, her anxieties were growing.

'Still, it's better to have him here,' Ally hastened to reassure her. 'That is to say, under close observation.'

'I agree. He's so polite to me, but I'm uncertain if it's sincere. He has a moustache!'

'Does that say something to you?' Ally queried.

'I've never liked moustaches. I think they're sneaky. They make me think of villains. I'm not happy with beards, either.'

'He hasn't got a beard, has he?' Ally was starting to get

a mental picture, and it didn't look good.

'No, he's very nice-looking. Very well groomed. Not a man's man, if you know what I mean. He likes chatting with the ladies.'

'Nothing wrong with that,' Ally said breezily. 'As a rule, I'm drawn to men who enjoy women's company. Why don't we sit back and relax, and give Mr Keppler a fair go?'

'My sentiments exactly,' Susan agreed with a twinkle. 'By the way, Sacha and I are a bit nervous of bringing failure down on our heads. We've elected you party organiser.'

'Oh, no, you don't,' Ally exclaimed, startled.

'You'll be wonderful!' Susan dismissed her objection quite cheerfully. 'You're a born organiser, Ally. I don't think one can actually learn it. You know exactly how to handle the staff. Even Mrs Tanner is in the habit of consulting you.'

'That's because she gets my attention,' Ally explained patiently.

'That's right,' Susan insisted. 'You're the true Leo, a born leader.'

'That's wonderful!' Ally gave a wry little moan. 'Leos get all the work.'

'We'll help,' Susan offered primly. 'You're the general. We're the troops. It will be the best party we've ever had. Kiall is taking us all into Brisbane eight sharp on Tuesday morning, and you're going to dress me to the nines. I've got tons of cash I've never touched. I want us all to look marvellous.'

'Oh, you will!' Ally agreed faintly.

'We'll have a marvellous lunch. I'll break my diet for one meal. We'll make a real day of it.'

'What does Kiall have to say about my being party organiser?' Ally asked. 'Or doesn't he know?'

'You know Kiall knows everything,' Susan teased. 'I

walked into his study, he was working on his papers, and I told him you were going to handle the party. He said, "I believe it." Just like that. *I believe it.* In fact, he didn't even look up.'

'So, how many guests are we having? What's my budget?' Ally asked.

'I'm sure Kiall doesn't care. Just do it right!'

In all, a hundred people were invited, a small crowd by Outback standards. Mowana homestead, its guest bungalows and the staff quarters could not fully accommodate the overnight guests, so it was arranged that neighbouring properties would help out, as was normal for one of Mowana's legendary weekends.

The day in Brisbane was a frantic rush. Under Ally's guidance, Susan, for probably the first time in her life, acted like a wealthy woman, spending money like water as she amassed a fitting wardrobe. She walked into the top hairdressers a pretty, middle-aged woman, and came out looking irresistibly chic. The years dropped from her with a cunning new hairstyle devised to show off her pretty neck and ears and lift her whole line. She was so delighted, Ally had to turn away and bite on her lip to banish the few sentimental tears that stung her eyes.

'It might sound crazy to you,' she whispered to Susan, 'but I think you should get Gino or one of his people out for the weekend. That means you'll look terrific all the time.'

'You ask. I couldn't.' Susan was still fingering her shining blonde hair, her blue eyes bright with pleasure.

Ally checked, and Gino himself pronounced himself available. Who wouldn't jump at a weekend on one of the country's historic stations with all expenses paid?

'Bring a friend,' Ally added. She thought he might be lonely.

'OK, I will! I've got this gorgeous new girlfriend!'

Ally's eyes filled with tears of joy.

She had been promising herself a couple of new outfits, and it was just as well she was an expert because, having offered to help Susan and Sacha with their choices, she could only spare her own selections a passing glance.

The boutique owner, an old friend, linked an arm around her waist. 'Time to try them on, darling?' Mischief gleamed in her spectacularly made-up eyes.

'They'll be perfect,' Ally whispered while Sacha chattered on. She indicated the three outfits with her hand. Two day dresses and a marvellous number for the Saturday night, black and gold with shoe-string straps.

'Count on it,' the woman laughed. 'You're a dream to fit. I'm tempted to give them to you for nothing with all this business. How about twenty per cent?'

'Done!'

Even Mrs Tanner had taken her day in the city very seriously. She had provided herself with a bag of sweets to help her through the flight, but Ally kept her so busy talking food and drink for the weekend that she was dumbfounded when it was time to land.

'You can't mean we're here?' She looked at Ally in absolute astonishment.

'No flutters?' Ally asked smilingly.

'Not one. I mean, it was so smooth and pleasant!'

'Then you could get to New Zealand?'

'What do you think?' Mrs Tanner asked with superb aplomb.

Leon and several other guests flew in by charter flight early Saturday morning. Sacha was so happy, she was incandescent, but Ally felt a little as if Judgement Day was at hand. She didn't want to be involved in Sacha's big romance, she didn't need the responsibility, but it was an important quality in a friend.

The homestead was looking magnificent. Ally had detailed station hands to help her rearrange the furniture, and she had stored a good many valuable, heavy pieces away. Over the long years so much had been acquired, antiques had to jostle each other for space. Now everything had room to breathe and be admired. She had even shifted the major paintings around, finding the most favourable spots. Elaborate drapery had been taken down, aired and dusted off. The chandeliers had been cleaned, a monumental task, but when switched on now sparkled gloriously. In fact, everything gleamed, sparkled, shone. Ally was nothing if not thorough.

To leave the home gardens looking their beautiful best, she had ordered masses of flowers to be flown in along with mountains of sea food: luscious lobsters, crayfish, crabs and prawns, freshly caught barramundi, the magnificent fish of the North. The station supplied its own prime beef, chicken, lamb and turkey, but fresh fruit and vegetables made up the cargo, including the finest strawberries money could buy. Mrs Tanner couldn't possibly handle all the catering, so Ally approached her diplomatically, giving her authority over additional staff sent from a Brisbane agency: chefs, waiters and maids. Far from worrying about what she was spending, Ally had a glorious time. Mowana needed this. She had languished too long. Characteristically, Ally saw the homestead as a beautiful woman, and she was giving her back her radiance.

Kiall appeared to be pleased—he certainly didn't stop her—although he continued to mark the many changes with a mocking uplifted eyebrow.

'You have a genius for this, Ally!' Susan praised her. 'How I envy you your confidence and fine eye.'

Ally went through the week on the heights, awarded

the temporary position of chatelaine of a great station. For a
girl who had been reared on a small farm, she thought she
was handling it pretty well. All one needed was verve,
nerve and plenty of somebody else's money. She wondered
what she was going to do when she was back on her own
salary!

Leon Keppler responded to their introduction with
practised grace of manner. Ally, who relied heavily on her
inherited Highland intuition, was not taken in by his efforts
to win her over. It was expected as Sacha's friend that she
would have influence over the younger girl, and Leon
moved to make her an ally as soon as possible.

But it didn't work. Ally didn't trust those deep, dark eyes.
They weren't brown but black, and besides, she was as
wary of his grip as of his overtures. She felt Kiall had made
a powerful point. Had she told him, for example, that a
long-lost uncle had left her a gold mine in South Africa, she
thought he might quickly overcome his desire for the much
younger Sacha. There were important differences between
them. The usual experience was to become involved with
one's peers, but Leon Keppler was far beyond Sacha's level
of development. Ally started to worry also about the extent
of their lovemaking. If a person was unscrupulous, man or
woman, one couldn't expect them to play fair in their sexual
behaviour. Dreams of getting married, setting up house and
playing wife and mother were one thing, but there were a
lot of details to be ironed out before Sacha, in particular,
could devote her energies to either role. Ally made the
decision that she had better have a little talk with Sacha.
Thus far, Susan hadn't. There was a decided tendency to
evade things there, but Susan was a sweet person. Ally
fitted more the role of mentor, with strong opinions about
just about everything. Her worries increased as she
considered Leon Keppler might well try to force the

situation—in other words, catch the prize by fair means or foul. He would have to put the Pacific Ocean between himself and his would-be stepbrother-in-law if he did. Kiall Lancaster was a man one simply didn't cross.Unless there was a considerable fortune at stake, and there was!

'Isn't this thrilling?' Sacha whispered in Ally's ear. 'Doesn't Leon look handsome? Did you ever see anyone so frightfully elegant? I'm so happy to see him, you have no idea.'

'Sacha tells me you are responsible for the weekend's festivities,' Leon praised her in his dark honey voice. 'The homestead looks magnificent!' He nodded his sleek, dark head as he looked around. 'There were moments when I wanted to take to it myself. I see you've shifted the big Streeton. It looks splendid there. Such an outstanding collection. One of the three finest private collections in the country, but it desperately needs someone well qualified to look after it. I offered to do it from the very start. One should be allowed to get on with it, wouldn't you agree?'

'I agree it's vital for the paintings to be housed properly and have a restorer in from time to time,' Ally agreed politely.

'Of course, I was Mr Lancaster's first choice,' Leon assured her, an ultra-smooth character in his fashionable clothes. An impeccably tended moustache graced his top lip, not the Magnum variety, but more the second lead in the old movies. Unlike Susan, Ally thought she could handle it. He looked arrestingly urbane, but not exactly true blue. He travelled frequently, several times overseas, mostly London, where he had established the best contacts for his business. It had to be said he was extremely knowledgeable about art, and a genuine lover of all things beautiful. Ally formed the opinion that that included himself. He wasn't at all the sort of person she could have welcomed happily as Sacha's beau, but she had to admit she could happily see him as a suitable escort for Karen Fulbrook. In a way, they were two of a kind.

Luncheon was a magnificent alfresco affair with dozens of tables and chairs set out on the lawn, shaded from the hot sun by a variety of striped and fringed umbrellas. Two huge marquees, food—pink and white, drink—blue and white, drew the crowds who were beautifully turned out and in the best of spirits. Everybody knew just about everyone else, and there was a good deal of betting on the outcome of the polo match scheduled for three o'clock that afternoon. The gala party would begin at eight with all-night dancing. Two bands had been hired for the occasion and specially flown out. Mowana was *en fête*.

Ally, in a beautiful, featherlight, yellow crêpe-de-Chine dress and a white picture hat weighed down with yellow roses, was directing a waiter towards a certain table when a familiar voice spoke unpleasantly at her elbow.

'What a meteoric rise in society, Miss Allen. I honestly don't think I've seen anyone close the gap so rapidly.'

Ally turned sharply, dismayed by the tone. 'For heaven's sake,' she exclaimed crisply, 'don't you ever let up?'

Karen, looking extremely attractive in a three-piece silk ensemble in black and white, with a stylish black boater, was staring at her with glittering eyes. 'That applies equally to you. It's a little unusual, isn't it, to have the visitor play hostess?'

'Hardly the hostess; I'm a working girl,' Ally said.

'Of course, Mother spotted you at once. She thought you even more stunning than your reputation. Mother likes to admire our enemies in some way. It makes our little battles so much more fun.'

'Try battling with me and you might finish in hospital,' Ally said tartly. 'You could tell Mother that as well. You aren't the only ones who know how to work themselves into the spirit of the thing. I know you've earned a reputation for being fiercely competitive, most likely instilled by Mother, but I've had it right from the horse's mouth. The affair between you and Kiall is over.'

'So how come I'm here?' Karen asked triumphantly.

'Evidently you're suffering some form of neurosis.' Ally shrugged. 'Look, I'm happy to call a truce, Karen, if you will.'

'Truce? Never!' Karen reacted as though the thought had never occurred to her. 'You're the one who's going to back out.'

'No problem. I never stay where I'm not wanted.'

Ally could see there was nothing to be gained by reasonable discussion. Karen had repeatedly overcome years of competition, was it any wonder she was hanging in one more time? It was pushing persistence to its limits, but maybe it would work.

Leon noticed her immediately as she skirted the blue and white striped marquee. 'How goes it?' he asked smoothly, giving her a friendly smile.

'Swimmingly,' she said casually. 'And you, enjoying yourself?'

'I always do on this place. It's splendid, isn't it? A million wild acres, and Lancaster king of all he surveys. My little Sacha didn't get too much of his arrogance.'

'Can't you rephrase that?' Ally looked up at him, eyes gleaming.

'Certainly.' Something moved in his dark eyes, like fish in a murky pond. 'Trememdous self-assurance, I mean. I don't think one ever really acquires it, no matter how successful one might become. It's something that come with being born to the silver, so to speak. A kind of bred-in-the-bone, unshakeable self-confidence.'

'I'd call it the confidence of achievement,' Ally suggested mildly.

'Of course. May I compliment you on your outfit?' Leon swiftly changed an unwieldy subject. 'It's truly beautiful, as are you.'

'Why, thank you.' Ally gave him her professional smile.'

'I couldn't help noticing you were talking to Karen . . . Fulbrook, isn't it? Attractive creature. She reminds me of a little Parisienne.'

She does have that air,' Ally agreed. 'So chic. Dark and petite. The millions help.'

A sharp pause. 'Really?'

'Oh, yes,' Ally said, watching him closely.

'I didn't think her family had as much as that,' he said, stroking his moustache.

Ally took a deep breath. 'Some multi-millionaires like to keep a low profile, but it all came out as we girls were chatting. Karen is going to be a very rich woman one of these days.'

'Money does marry money, doesn't it?' Leon snorted, almost with disgust.

'Marrying? Who's she marrying?' Ally asked with wide, guileless eyes. 'This is news.'

'Surely it's Lancaster, for God's sake?' His dark brows sagged in a frown.

'Nooo!' Ally gave him a pitying smile. 'That was all over years ago.'

'Are you sure?' Leon looked completely unconvinced. 'I understood they were at the stage of announcing their engagement.'

'I assure you that's not true.' Ally turned her head and looked discreetly about. 'I don't usually trade information, but as you're Sacha's friend . . .'

'Please. Believe me, what you tell me, my lips are sealed.'

'I've discussed this with Kiall.'

'No!' His dark eyes narrowed and he stared at her admiringly. 'Maybe he's never met anyone as beautiful as you before.'

'It's not that.' Ally fingered her long row of pearls. 'He told me he never had any intention of marrying Karen, at any stage, and that was that. I know there's been a lot of gossip. Most of it, I suspect, put about by Karen and her family, but one can't count the chickens before they're hatched.'

Leon looked down at his double-breasted classic blazer. 'That's the way he treats all his women,' he said almost sneeringly. 'If he didn't want an heir for all this, I don't suppose he'd marry at all. After all, he can get all he wants without offering marriage.'

'You sound as though you very much disliked him,' Ally said coolly.

'Not at all,' Leon hastened to assure her. 'I admire him tremendously. Who wouldn't? But if ever a man had *droit de seigneur* written all over him, it's Lancaster. He could make a fortune in the movies if he had to. So damned big and handsome, and all that machismo. Is there a thing the man lacks?'

Ally looked back at him without blinking. 'The love of a good woman?'

Leon showed his fine teeth again in a laugh. 'Am I to conclude you're interested in him?'

'He'd probably hate to hear it, but he must be one of the most eligible bachelors in the country.'

'And it's not Karen?' Leon's smiling stare was as searching as a beacon.

'She's waiting for the next man to come along,' Ally told him firmly. 'I'd say she was ready to be swept off her feet. Women are so much more vulnerable, aren't they, when a long attachment is over? Then, she must be nearly thirty. It can be a terrifying age!'

'True.' Leon appeared to be giving a lot of thought to this. 'We've only met briefly, and I got the impression that she didn't approve of my friendship with Sacha.'

'Somehow you two do look a litle mismatched!' Ally smiled sweetly and hastened on, 'Only in the sense that you're so much more sophisticated. Probably Karen would like to see you with someone . . . well, someone more like . . . herself? One can't help marking the difference. It's important a couple should be at the same mental and emotional level, wouldn't you say?'

Leon was staring at her very hard. 'You're Sacha's friend. What do you think?'

'I'm not interfering at all,' Ally lied though her teeth. 'I know Sacha believes she cares a great deal about you.'

'She does,' Leon asserted, almost threateningly.

'I'm sure, but for now I'm thinking about you. Don't you think you'd be a whole lot happier with a woman of your own standing? This is an important decision in your life.'

'I've had Lancaster to contend with,' Leon pointed out bitterly. 'He disapproves of our friendship, that's for sure. The only thing that surprises me is that he has invited me out here.'

'Maybe he's done you a favour in more ways than one.' Ally looked over her shoulder, smiling wryly. 'There's Karen now, looking a little lost. Why don't you go over and say hello? I have to go in search of Mrs Tanner.'

'Why not?' Leon reacted like an actor working himself into a new role. 'I've lived through a broken romance. I might be of some help.'

Sacha will kill me, Ally thought. And quite rightly.

Ally walked away, feeling troubled, until a bright young

voice called her name. It was Sacha, looking very flushed and pretty, the centre of an animated group of young men.

'Come over here, Ally, and meet my friends.'

Ally went smilingly, and the young men jumped to their feet, their expressions of admiration unanimous.

'Wow!' a young man called Bruce exclaimed for all of them. 'Is this what's meant by bringing high fashion to the Outback?'

'Like it?' Obligingly, Ally twirled.

'Terrific!'

Another young man spun around, trying to locate a free chair, but Ally shook her head. 'I'd love to join you, perhaps later on. I have a few more things to organise, then I can relax.'

'Ally, you remember me talking about Mark McCarthy.' Sacha smiled radiantly up at her. 'Mark has been overseas for twelve months.'

'Of course.' Ally couldn't remember, but she gave the tall and dashing blond, blue-eyed young man her hand. 'How are you, Mark?'

'Absolutely delighted to meet you.' He bowed over her hand. 'Sacha told me you were someone special.'

'She is to me.'

'I know. Sacha's a darling! Mark McCarthy reached for Sacha's hand. 'I was bowled over when I saw how much she'd grown up. She was only a little pea-brained Shirley Temple when we used to play together.'

'Pea-brained?' Sacha hit him, giggling.

'Sure. I spent my time taking care of you. Don't you remember?'

'I do.' Sacha blushed. 'Mark's father managed one of our properties, Mala Downs,' she explained to Ally, so Ally could make the connection. 'I saw a lot of Mark in the old days. Until he turned into a gangling teenager and had to be sent away to boarding-school.'

'I'm a fully qualified solicitor now. Still taking care of other people's problems.' He smiled with attractive openness.

'Mark is playing in the polo match this afternoon,' Sacha told Ally proudly.

'I'm not an eight-handicap like Kiall,' Mark protested. 'He's magnificent, my idol! Major Dawson, you know Major Dawson?'

Ally nodded her amber head, and the wide white brim of her hat dipped.

'He always says Kiall could be the world's greatest player if he took himself as seriously as, say, the Argentinians. We have our endless savannahs like the pampa. Mowana has a great polo field, and Kiall can well afford a string of polo ponies. It's a rich man's sport.'

'And I would have thought . . . dangerous?' Ally asked, with her own anxieties.

'Fastest game in the world!' Mark grinned. 'You're in for a wonderful time this afternoon, Ally. And you'd better bet on our team. Kiall is the most marvellous captain a team could ever have. His performance on the field lifts us all. Major Dawson's nephew, Barry Wentworth, is the captain of the other team. He's a great player, no less than a six-goal handicap. But the teams are pretty evenly matched. That's polo's special charm. A minus-two player, that is to say, a beginner, can get to play with a man like Kiall. But not this afternoon. I'd have to say in all modesty, we're all strong players.'

'Mark is super,' Sacha said with a shining light in her blue eyes. 'I just hope his usual recklessness doesn't come against him. I couldn't bear to see him fall.'

'All in the game, hey, fellas?' Mark glanced around his friends, all of them looking blissfully unconcerned. 'That guy over there, Paul Hilton, he's our bad boy. He invariably comes off.'

'We'll see, McCarthy,' his friend warned. 'You've been the victim of my ruthless play more than once.'

What was happening around here? Ally thought. How could Sacha love Leon Keppler when she was blossoming like a flower under Mark McCarthy's cobalt-blue regard? What was all the brooding about Leon? The intense preoccupation with getting him out here? And for what? While Leon stood in apparently deep conversation with Karen Fulbrook, Sacha was staring up at Mark McCarthy as if he was the centre of her life. Did it illustrate the perversity of youth, the capacity for rapid change? One thing about Sacha, she didn't easily fit into a pattern.

The polo field was looking splendid, thanks to a good deal of attention. Roughly twice as long as it was wide, it was bounded by sideboards about a foot high, with goal-posts spaced eight yards apart at either end of the field. Most of the ladies had changed from their luncheon finery into garments more sporting, but Ally didn't think anybody could match the sheer dash of the players and the splendour of the thoroughbred and near-thoroughbred horses in their white and yellow leg boots. Kiall led his team on to the field, a striking figure in navy and white jersey, white breeches, white helmet, knee guards and glossy black boots. Everyone shouted and cheered, a happy, united community intent on enjoying a fast and thrilling game.

'Doesn't he look *gorgeous?*' A young woman behind Ally hissed to her partner. 'I can't understand how someone like Kiall wasn't married long ago. Karen, for instance, though she leaves me cold.'

Ally allowed herself a moment of empathy. Barry Wentworth and his team were now trotting on to the field,

their jerseys white with a green emblem, the helmets black.
Again the good-natured cheering went up. Everyone had
placed a bet, with the proceeds to go to charity.

'There's Mark,' Sacha whispered to Ally. So much for
Leon on her other side! 'I do hope he's not going to get to
get himself into any trouble. He's very reckless, you know.'

'Like to let me in on your little secret?' Leon asked
suavely out of the blue.

'Nothing, darling.' Sacha smiled back at him brilliantly.
'I was just pointing out some of the players.'

'That Mark someone, the handsome blond giant?' Leon
asked acidly.

'He is playing,' Sacha nodded. 'Oh, look. There's Paul!'

Ally felt like shaking her head in wonderment, as it was,
she kept her eyes glued on the field. She had read all she
could about the game of polo, so she knew the rules were
somewhat similar to those of hockey. There were four
players to each team, the first two players playing
offensively, the third and fourth playing back. Each
playing-period was called a chukka; there could be six or, as
today, eight chukkas to the match, and each chukka was
seven minutes long. Four-minute intervals were allowed
between chukkas to change ponies, and there was a ten-
minute break half-time. The game was thought to have
originated in Persia about 600 BC. But the modern game
had its origin in India in the mid-1800s, when a group of
British officers copied the sport from tribal horsemen and
introduced such niceties as rules. A white willow-root ball
was a big improvement on a human skull, and four players
to a team was less hazardous than playing an entire tribe.
Since then, the game had become international. Prince
Philip and later Prince Charles, coached by the great
Australian player Sinclair Hill, had done a great deal to
popularise the sport, not only in England but, through

their illustrious standing, the whole world of sportsmen who identified with horses, and lightning-fast ball games with that tantalising whiff of danger.

It was the danger that worried Ally now, and she remembered reading the Princess of Wales had similar anxieties when she saw her husband ride on to the field. There was no doubt about the frequent and spectacular falls and the duels between powerful riders and trained animals.

Further around the semicircle of spectators, Susan and Major Dawson sat with several other important guests. All of them were clapping the umpire, who ran on to the field to place the white willow-root ball. Susan had never looked better in her life, and Ally studied her with considerable pleasure and satisfaction. She hadn't been exaggerating when she said she could transform Susan with her professional know-how. Susan looked so youthful and charming, so flawlessly turned out, quite a number of people had failed to recognise her at first. Not that Susan appeared to care. Her gaze was drawn magnetically to Major Dawson, who appeared delighted to be given the slightest encouragement. It looked very much as if happiness for Susan was just around the corner. Major Dawson was such a gorgeous man, so kind and tolerant and understanding, with such a good sense of humour. It didn't hurt, either, that he was so distinguished in appearance and obviously ready to devote his life to some fortunate woman.

'Mum looks wonderful, doesn't she?' Sacha squeezed Ally's arm. 'God bless her! She looks as if she's had a face-lift. I'm sure that old battleaxe Mrs Fulbrook didn't recognise her. She was so full of stutters and stammers! I half hoped she'd choke. You're so good, Ally, you should start up an agency of your own. You really know how to make other women look good. Not only that, feel good. Mum looks a million dollars, a real doll. Major Dawson has never taken his eyes off her.'

'What are you two nattering about?' Leon leaned forward, giving his faintly smarmy smile to cover his intense irritation.

'Girl-talk,' Sacha said brightly. 'Don't worry, Leon. Look, they're off! Poor old Barry will have a battle trying to eliminate Kiall. It's going to be interesting watching his tactics to try and slow Kiall down. His speed is remorseless!'

A slight understatement, Ally thought. It was devastating! Repeatedly throughout the first half, Ally found her heart in her throat. She was not qualified to make informed comment on the game, but it was the easiest possible task to name the most outstanding player. There was such a quality of excitement in Kiall's game. No other player was able to match his speed and power, nor his range of strokes, which Sacha proudly assured her was complete. It was a lightning-fast field and there were many times when Ally thought Kiall woud be dismounted as Barry Wentworth barged in steeply and hard.

She thought the magnificent horses needed great courage with all the barging and bumping, the miraculously fast twists and turns. Kiall's black stallion, in particular, an ex-racehorse called Khan, gave every appearance of relishing the battle as much as his master. Both apparently had only one thought: to win. In four chukkas he had slammed in eight goals against the opposing team's best defence, so now the atmosphere was of increasing desperation on the part of Barry Wentworth's team.

The ten-minute intermission passed in a flash. Ally saw Karen Fulbrook rush across to Kiall, and then her brother whispering words of praise and encouragement. Ally remained seated while Leon brought the girls long, frosted drinks. The Fulbrook brother, Alan, who had taken one fall and remounted so swiftly that everyone cheered, bore a striking resemblance to his sister, except that where she was petite he was at least six foot, and so attractive he had his own female following.

'This is a sport for the real élite,' Leon drawled, with a strong suggestion of envy. 'How could the average sportsman hope to keep a string of polo ponies?'

Such overt bitterness surprised Ally. 'It might be expected to be easier out here,' she pointed out reasonably. 'How could you separate Mowana and horses? All the players, I believe, were reared on properties. I would think that was vital. The Outback is man and his horse. You could say all the raw material is readily available, the land and the ponies.'

'God knows why they want to try to kill themselves.' Leon dropped languidly into his seat. 'It looks terribly dangerous to me.'

'Could be.' Ally was thinking the same thing herself.

Sacha, with cheeks flushed, didn't appear to be listening. Instead she was staring across the field to where Mark McCarthy was checking the girth of his new pony. A very pretty young girl ran towards him and threw her arms around his neck.

'Can you beat that!' Sacha muttered.

'What is it?' Ally made the lightning decision to draw Leon Keppler's attention. It might help him realise Sacha was so young that she was still in the process of change. 'What does Tracy Durham think she's doing?'

'I would have thought that was obvious,' Leon said in grim tones. 'What are you sounding so injured about?'

Sacha settled back. 'I didn't expect her to make such a spectacle of herself. She's a real lightweight.'

'She's very pretty,' Ally pointed out fairly.

'Do you think so?' Sacha regarded her friend with a very

injured expression.

Ally nodded. 'But not as pretty as you.'

'I wonder what your interest in that young man is?' Leon asked in a dangerously smooth tone.

'I've known him all my life.' Sacha smiled bleakly, trying desperately to unwind.

'You're my girl, and don't forget it!' Leon leaned over possessively and kissed her flushed cheek. 'Ten dollars that young man comes off. He's reckless to the point of stupidity.'

'Come on, Mowana!' Sacha shrieked. The teams had remounted now and were coming back on to the field.

Leon Keppler kept his hypnotic black eyes fastened on Mark McCarthy right through the second half, so much so that Ally felt like standing up and blocking horse and rider from his line of sight. Barry Wentworth's team, which included Mark, were playing more furiously as they tried to combat the opposing captain's blazing turn of speed. At one point it weas a dangerous mêlée, with the white ball rolling beneath the ponies' hooves, until Alan Fulbrook got in a good shot, driving the ball well upfield. Kiall and his black stallion, Khan, almost on its haunches, wheeled and tore along the line after it, avoiding all defence and hammering a goal home.

The crowd went wild, cries of adoration and support soaring to the peacock skies.

'This is pathetic!' Leon cried comtemptuously. 'No one is giving Lancaster a match.'

'What would you know?' Sacha turned on him, blue eyes blazing. 'The others are playing beautifully. Kiall's so damned good.'

'Isn't that what I'm saying?' Leon answered angrily. 'He's winning the match on his own.'

'Barry and Mark will get serious, don't you worry. No

one expected them to win, but they're definitely in there.'

Just as she said it Barry Wentworth got the head of his mallet on the white ball and, with a full, furious swing that kept all the other riders back, thundered in a brilliant goal.

'Good show!' Sacha roared.

'Whose side are you on?' Leon demanded. 'I would have thought your brother could call on your support.'

By this time, everyone on the opposing team was trying to disrupt Kiall's play. It could have been a rough-house, but the umpire was alert and Kiall and his splendid pony were unbelievably tough. It stupefied Ally, the amount of stamina that was required, and Kiall had a headstart with his height and physical strength. Stunning as he was at any time, he looked godlike on horseback.

Barry Wentworth, with far more finesse than the rest of his team, played very much better in the closing minutes, chalking up three more goals. By this time Sacha's cries of encouragement were pealing around the grounds, so much so that Mark McCarthy, evidently hearing them, was driven into trying to perform a miracle. He gave a joyous war cry, changed angle very sharply, gathered himself, leaned sideways off his pony and lifted his stick aloft. So concentrated was he on making contact with the white ball, he was unprepared for the collision with Alan Fulbrook's fearless pony.

Sacha's piercing, panicked scream coincided with Mark's flying through the air.

'Oh, my God!' Ally pressed her hands together over her heart. This was a thrilling match, no doubt about it, but she didn't think she could stand seeing someone injured.

Like the trained athlete he was, Mark rolled with the fall and, as a stunned hush fell over the ground, he seemed to bounce like a gymnast, then sprang up with his two feet planted firmly on the turf. Another two seconds and, to a renewed burst of cheering, he had hauled himself back into the saddle.

'Young idiot!' Leon exclaimed, making it sound like a curse. 'It's a wonder the lot of them aren't paraplegics.'

Ally looked quickly at Sacha. 'Are you all right?'

Sacha had gone very white.

'No,' she said. 'I feel sick.'

'Put your head down,' Ally advised. 'Keep it down like a good girl. The feeling will pass.'

Her brother at that moment was engaged in scoring the final and winning goal.

'I don't understand this,' Leon said sharply.

'Can't it wait till Sacha feels better?' Ally fixed him with a lioness's eyes.

'Sacha, darling.' Leon changed the quality of his response. 'Allow me to take you back up to the house. No harm was done to your friend.'

Susan, who had been clapping delightedly, now caught sight of Ally bent protectively over her daughter. She leapt to her feet and rushed over towards them, followed by Major Dawson.

'Ally, what's the matter?' Susan looked at Ally, shocked.

'I'm all right, Mum.' Sacha's voice was wan and muffled.

'She'll be OK in a moment,' Ally said soothingly. 'A combination of the heat and excitement.'

'Darling!' Leon jumped up so that Susan could take his seat beside Sacha. 'My poor little girl.'

Sacha lifted her head, the colour coming back into her cheeks. 'I've got to see Mark,' she said.

Susan looked astonished, as well she might. 'Mark, darling?' She gave a flustered little laugh.

'Yes, Mark. I got such a fright, I'm not thinking straight.'

Ally thought the opposite. Sacha's thinking was telling.

'I'll be damned,' Leon Keppler said smoothly, but his dark eyes looked bemused.

'I think she should go back to the house. Lie down for a half-hour,' Ally suggested. 'It was shocking when Mark fell. I know I had my heart in my mouth.'

Somehow Sacha was lead away, and Ally was called on to present the impressive silver trophy to the captain of the winning team.

Amid cheers and clapping and whistles, Kiall bent his handsome dark head and kissed Ally's cheek. 'What the devil is going on with Sacha?' he murmured against Ally's temple.

'Nothing for you to worry about. I think she's now decided she's in love with Mark McCarthy.'

'What?' His head jerked back. His silver eyes flashed as brightly as the cup.

'Smile, Mr Lancaster. These are all your fans.'

Kiall not only smiled, he made a gracious and witty speech, his natural quality of leadership and splendid horsemanship cooling the heat of the game. Barry Wentworth spoke and was applauded, and while everyone looked on, Kiall unexpectedly linked his arm around Ally's narrow waist, drew her to his lean, powerful body and, apparently carried away by the enthusiasm of the moment, dropped a kiss on her lovely amber head. She couldn't move either, because he continued to keep his arm around her.

Ten paces away, three pairs of dark eyes were drilling holes in her. Karen, her brother Alan, and a tiny but very awesome-looking lady who could only be Mrs Fulbrook.

'You can let me go now,' Ally murmured to Kiall sweetly, her upturned mouth with the sheen of a rose.

'That's OK. I like holding you.'

'Don't think you're using me as a shield.'

'My dear girl, I thought I was wearing you like a beautiful

ornament on my arm.'

'Can't you see your old friends the Fulbrooks?' she challenged.

Kiall's brilliant gaze changed direction, and he laughed aloud. 'I suppose all families stick together.'

'I don't think I've met anyone quite like them. They think I've stolen you away.'

'And haven't you?' He stared down at her with a quizzical gleam in his eyes.

'You're suffering from sunstroke!'

He was still studying her. 'Why did you change your outfit?' he asked finally. 'I've never seen a woman look so ravishing in my whole life. The colour and that hat dipping down over your face. I'm going to have to ask you to wear it again.'

'And I'm going to have t ask you to stop playing games!' Ally retaliated by placing her hand over his and digging her long, enamelled nails into his tanned skin. 'Don't expect hero-worship from me.'

His disturbing mouth curved into a smile. 'Sometimes you say things you don't mean.' He released her very gently, turning as a friend saluted him. 'Hi, there, Garry——'

It was Ally's moment to escape.

CHAPTER EIGHT

IT WAS the most amazing time Ally had ever had. There were people everywhere—in the homestead, on the verandas, in the garden—all over them bent on having a glorious time. She found herself rushing to her room to change back into her beautiful yellow dress. Pleasing Kiall appeared to be the name of the game. She turned in her bedroom and surveyed her willowy figure. She had never truly looked at herself as a woman, or as a sex-object, until now. A top model, certainly, a product for the heady world of high fashion. Now she looked at herself as a desirable female. Kiall had done that to her, shattering her defences into a million fragments. She was very fortunate in having a beautiful skin and good healthy hair, but surely she hadn't always had this . . . this . . . aura, this allure?

She truly felt as voluptuous as a rose, with its beauty and fragrance on display. She looked into the mirror. Her eyes were huge, golden and full of fire. There was a natural apricot flush on her cheekbones. Even her skin had an added lustre, its texture like a baby's. There was a great difference between her normal working-face and the face of a woman in love. Now that she really thought about it, she considered she had to look twice as good. The truly unsettling thing about being a woman was needing a man to realise one's full potential. She had another dress she had intended to wear in this early-evening period, for the gala party would not start until eight o'clock, but the fact Kiall that liked this dress was all the incentive she needed to put it back on.

The colour was lovely. Sometimes she thought that this particular shade of yellow was the best colour of all for her.

She was so full of excitement, she couldn't believe it.

'Keep cool, Ally,' she cautioned herself. 'You might be madly in love with the man, but you don't have to show it.'

In the kitchen, Mrs Tanner was issuing orders like a five-star general.

'Everything all right here, Mrs Tanner?'

Mrs Tanner came forward, visibly sweetening her expression. 'Everything going very much as planned, Miss Alison,' she said cheerfully. She always called Ally 'Miss Alison', something she had decided on herself. 'You're happy?

'You're doing a marvellous job, Mrs Tanner,' Ally complimented her.

Mrs Tanner bent her eyes on a certain person. 'A few little squabbles. I soon broke them up. There can only be one boss. Everyone has eaten so much, I don't know how they're going to fit in supper tonight.'

'Oh, they will, I'm sure,' Ally said smilingly. 'It's amazing what the young men in particular can put away.'

'Just you leave everything to me,' Mrs Tanner told her supportively. 'I've never had so much fun in my life.'

Used to male admiration as a matter of course, Ally was scarcely aware of her own growing entourage. Obviously, mem married women who would make good wives and mothers, but they couldn't help chasing the glamour girls. It was some sort of status symbol and better than a Rolls. It was something she was used to, but not something that she needed. Ally took her own stunning looks very much for granted, a gift from God. This endeared her to photographers, who found her very easy to work with. Quite apart from her physical endowments, it was her professionalism and lack of temperament that had contributed to her meteoric rise. There were several photographers from the media invited for the weekend, and Ally had already posed any number of times and places on her own, with guests, and of course with her charismatic host.

Now Alan Fulbrook began to chase her around, showering her with compliments. She gathered she was glorious, totally contradicting his sister's opinion.

'You haven't met my mother yet, have you?'

Ally tried to keep her face expressionless. 'I haven't had that pleasure.'

Dark eyes moved from her creamy face to her throat and then to her breasts. 'Those are beautiful pearls.'

'A Christmas present to myself.'

'Really?' He looked highly sceptical.

'Yes, really. I got a kick out of it.'

Mrs Fulbrook was waiting for them with thin, smiling lips.

'Ah, Miss Allen.' she called as Ally approached. 'I've been so wanting to meet you.' Seated, she looked very tiny, but she had the presence of a duchess.

'Mrs Fulbrook.' Ally had to stoop to take the bejewelled, outstretched hand.

'My daughter has told me so much about you.'

'I'm sure she has.' Ally smiled sweetly.

'Alan, you may leave us.' Mrs Fulbrook dismissed her tall, good-looking son with a wave of her hand.

'I'm coming back!' He gave Ally a hot conspiratorial smile.

'Please sit down, Miss Allen.' Drusilla Fulbrook gestured to the adjoining rattan chair with a languid hand.

'For a few moments,' Ally agreed pleasantly. 'It's been a marvellous day, hasn't it?'

'Indeed. You've quite stolen the show from poor Susan and Sacha.'

What did I expect? Ally thought. 'That was never the intention,' she answered quietly. 'I do hope you're not going to be unkind.'

'My dear Miss Allen, I'm anything I wish to be.'

'Then there's something I must tell you.' Ally gave her an unconcerned glance. 'I don't have to listen.' She stood up.

'Running away?' The venom overflowed.

'I do it all the time,' Ally returned briskly.

'Did my daughter tell you you're making us all dreadfully unhappy?' Mrs Fulbrook challenged.

'Please don't blame me for your problems, Mrs Fulbrook. They were well in place before you ever met me.'

'You're content to take somebody else's man?'

'I'm afraid that's one of your family's manias. In any case, you ought to know Kiall Lancaster well enough to know he makes his own decisions about everything. He's a very strong and independent man.'

'He has also had a long-term relationship with my daughter.'

'And I sympathise with her in a strange way, but I can't alter anything, Mrs Fulbrook, as you must well know. Whatever the relationship between them, it's none of my business.'

'Then why don't you stay out of it?' Drusilla Fulbrook demanded harshly.

'If it comes to that, why are *you* interfering?' Ally retaliated. 'Kiall would have to be the last man in the world to tolerate an interfering mother-in-law.'

For a moment, the formidable Mrs Fulbrook seemed robbed for words. 'I'd be more careful, Miss Allen, if I were you. Insolence from young people is not something I'm used to.'

'You initiated this unpleasantness, Mrs Fulbrook, not I. I had been told you were a real character.'

An outraged face looked back at her, red mantling the pale, matt cheeks. 'And I've been told you're nothing but a cheap adventuress. We all know women like you are always after money.'

'Well, it does come in handy.' Ally didn't deign to be

serious. 'You will excuse me?'

'With pleasure!' Mrs Fulbrooks's small nostrils flared. A memorable sight. 'I just want you to know you've made an enemy.'

'Thank you. I'll tell Kiall. He'll take care of it.'

Ally walked away very fast. The world was full of awful people. Just awful. They had no code of decency at all.

'What are you looking so het up about?' A long arm shot out of the open study and pulled Ally through the french doors.

Ally looked up at Kiall with accusing eyes, angered anew by his blazing good looks. 'It's not easy being a friend of the family around here,' she said shortly.

'And what does that mean?' He moved her so that they were out of sight.

'Are you willing to marry Karen or not?'

'What?' His breath was impatient, slow-drawn. He put his hands on her shoulders. 'I thought you knew. I'm not willing to marry anyone.'

'Then you've got to be some kind of freak,' she said snappily.

'Do you think so?' From the lightning flash in his eyes, she had made him angry.

'I mean, what's the problem?' She tilted her chin. 'You're thirty-four. You're handsome, intelligent, healthy. What more do you want?'

'Lady, a lot more than Karen, that's for sure.'

'Then why don't you tell her?'

Another flash in her eyes. 'Don't hassle me, Alison,' he said through his gritted teeth.

'Why not?' There was something crazy bubbling inside her. A wildness. 'You're complicating my life. I've just met Karen's charming mother.'

'That awful bitch,' Kiall said raspingly.

'Believe me, I know. She accused me of being an adventuress, for God's sake. Is anyone called an adventuress these days?'

'I can think of a few other words.'

'Well, lets's hear them,' she flared.

'Hot-head would be one.' He shook her. 'Can't you keep your voice down?'

'I'm sorry.' Incredibly, tears rushed into her eyes. 'If it isn't enough to get insulted by your girlfriend, her mother and her cocky brother, I have to shut up about it as well.'

'That's if you're capable of it.' Kiall pulled her to him with all his dark, frightening energy.

'You don't want to marry women, but occasionally you like to seduce them,' she said in a brittle, taunting voice.

'I haven't made it so far with you.'

'And you never will.'

There was a curious expression on his face—antagonism and a hard desire. 'You keep telling me that, Alison.'

'Might I remind you there are a hundred people surging around out there?' Her hands pushed back on his chest.

'Then if you're clever, you won't cry out.'

'You're suppose to be a hero.' She turned her head from side to side, knowing what he was about to do.

'Then why do you keep driving me to play the villain?'

'No, Kiall.' That shimmering sensuality was catching them in its web.

'Yes, Alison. I could kiss you silly every day.'

He lifted her amber head to him, his hand shaping her creamy nape beneath the thick silk of her hair. And all of a sudden, inexplicably, she went very quiet beneath his gaze. 'I need this,' he said in a very low, tense voice.

'I need it, too.' Shocked, Ally realised she had spoken.

He took her mouth very gently at first, a succession of brief, exploratory kisses that her own sensitive, satin lips couldn't resist. Her breath escaped in a fluttering sigh. She was utterly bemused, cradled almost like a baby against his taut, lean body. The nibbling, biting, questing kisses had her frantic. She went after him, straining for him, but he seemed determined on giving her just enough to drive her wild.

'You beast!' she cried, bereft.

'God, if I were I'd have had you a thousand times.'

'Why are you doing this to me?' He was a little rough with her, and arched her neck as his mouth slid down her throat.

'Could be I want to punish you for what you're doing to me,' he said tautly. 'You're beautiful, so beautiful. No one makes me so angry or gives me greater pleasure.'

His hand slid over her breast, and beneath his hand her heart was pounding.

'You have to stop, Kiall,' she whispered, her body coming alive with a hot, reckless urgency. The nipples of her breast were peaking against the yellow silk, and he moved his palm up and down over the excited tips.

'I know that.' But he still went on. 'Did you ever think, one of these times I'm not going to be able to stop?'

'Then I'd better arrange to go home.'

He jerked his head up and looked down at her beautiful, love-drugged face. 'What if I don't let you?'

'I have my life. You have yours.' She said it calmly, as if in control, but she looked incredibly soft and vulnerable.

'I gather you're saying you want that kind of life?'

'I have a lot of wants. Too many.' She was swamped by her feelings for him, but it was not in her nature to expose her hidden heart.

'I don't doubt that at all.' As suddenly as he had caught her to him, Kiall let her go, his handsome face darkening. 'If any of the Fulbrooks bother you at all, just let me know.'

Sacha came to her room as she was dressing for the party. Her smile contained an element of daring, as if she were a schoolgirl caught in some prank.

'Guess what?'

'You're in love with Mark McCarthy.'

Ally was sitting at the dressing-table, and Sacha swept forward, clamping a hand on Ally's bare shoulder. 'Is it as obvious as that?'

'Oh, my!' Ally said. 'Though women are angels, they do change their minds.'

'I thought I was in love with Leon.' Sacha plonked herself down on the sofa, spreading the voluminous folds of her flamingo-pink dress. Evidently she was resigned to her capricious nature. 'But he looks so staid beside Mark. Can you beat that? Staid! I never thought to see such a contrast!'

'Karen Fulbrook apparently doesn't mind the look of him,' Ally pointed out drily, perfecting the mascaraed sweep of her heavy, dark lashes.

'That's because Kiall has absolutely ignored her,' Sacha said piously. 'Not that she didn't set herself up for it. Some women just can't take no for an answer.'

'You're an interesting little soul yourself.'

'You think I've done the wrong thing?' Sacha was all wide-eyed innocence.

'Don't be embarrassed about it,' Ally said wryly. 'I think Leon Keppler will cope. But I suggest you don't try to lead Mark the same merry dance.'

'Oh, heavens, no!' Sacha stared back at her patiently. 'Mark and I played together as children. Are you nearly finished dressing? That black and gold is a knockout. I swear to God you've been the sensation of the day. I expect that's what's making Kiall cranky.'

'Kiall is cranky?' Ally asked acidly.

'I have an idea he's nuts about you, but he's not taking it too kindly.'

'He certainly is a puzzle,' said Ally drily.

'What about you, Ally?' Sacha met Ally's golden eyes very steadily.

'You know me!' Ally joked.

'I do know you. You're a very deep, serious person. What I would call a very responsible lady. How do you feel about Kiall?'

'Not a word to him?' Ally decided to be honest.

'I promise. Cross my heart.'

'I love him,' Ally said, suddenly looking at her long, glistening nails. 'I'm still trying to figure out how it happened.'

'Why not?' Sacha asked incredulously. 'You're made for each other. You're not worried about Karen, are you? She's no competition.'

'No, I'm not worried about Karen.' Ally swept up from the flounced seat. 'Kiall is another thing. He's not about to give anything away, and neither am I.'

'How earth-shaking!' Sacha cried. 'You'd make the most marvellous sister in the world.'

Ally bit down on her full lip. 'Never mind. We can still stay friends.' She stepped into her dress; it was cut like a slip, with a flare at the hem, gliding smoothly over her hips.

'Oh, that's gorgeous, smashing!' Sacha exclaimed, hands pressed together. 'Have you any idea how beautiful you are?'

'More importantly,' Ally said tartly, 'has Kiall?'

The party was reaching quite a pitch when someone suggested they have a treasure hunt.

'So, what's the treasure?' Susan cried delightedly, her face so full of life and colour, her figure so pert, she looked, at a little distance, hardly more than a teenager.

'I guess I can provide something,' Kiall promised. 'In fact, I've already got something planted. All our parties seem to end in a treasure hunt.'

'So, where is it?' Mark McCarthy called. 'House, garden, what?'

'House. The major rooms, including the verandas. Bedrooms off limits.' This was greeted by amused groans.

'You'll be my partner, won't you?' Alan Fulbrook, who had been quite persistent in his attentions, asked Ally, grabbing her hand.

'I don't think so. Party organiser should be around all the time.'

'What an excuse!' He threw back his dark head, crowing. 'You're not afraid of me, are you?'

'I find myself thinking, what's your game?'

'I can't believe it! And you so beautiful. Wouldn't any man in his right mind want to be with you?'

'I'm sorry, Alan,' Ally spoke as pleasantly as she could, to protect his sensibilities. 'You won't have any trouble finding someone else. I must be on hand in case Mrs Tanner needs me.'

'Supper's over,' he pointed out a little unpleasantly.

'Just about everyone is still drinking. Please excuse me.'

Ally went to turn away, but he kept a hard grip on her hand. 'You're one determined lady, aren't you?'

'Put it another way,' she said coolly, 'I make all my own decisions.'

'Perhaps you want to go wandering with someone else. Kiall, for instance?'

Ally shook her head. 'Please let me go.'

'What if I tell you I've heard some gossip that might concern you?'

'Gossip never concerns me, unless it's harmless and funny. I won't ask you again to let go of my hand.'

'What will you do? I can promise you I'd love anything.'

A tall man came to stand at his shoulder. 'A little confrontation?' Kiall's tone was light but steely.

'I was trying to persuade this gorgeous creature to join me on the treasure hunt.' Allan Fulbrook tried hard, but couldn't prevent hs quick flush.

'What a pity I need her to talk to a few people,' Kiall said suavely. 'There's Roslyn Palmer looking ardently in this direction.'

'If you don't mind, that's at you,' Alan pointed out bluntly.

'Then do me a favour. Partner her.'

'Oh, hell! It's Miss Allen I want.'

'I hate to depress you,' Kiall said smoothly, 'but you're wasting your time.'

'That's right, that's our Lancaster.' Alan gave him a faintly bitter salute. 'Catch you later, Allegra.'

'Don't have anything to do with him,' Kiall told Ally, almost curtly, as he escorted her back across the wide hallway.

'Do you mind! I handle admirers all the time.'

'I don't want you to have anything to do with him,' Kiall gritted, managing in the next instant to give a woman guest a charming smile.

'You're so dictatorial, it's disgusting. I know how to take care of myself.'

'May be some people, but the Fulbrooks aren't as well balanced as most.'

'Well, you should know.' Ally's great golden eyes flashed.

'Ally, aren't you coming?' Sacha shrieked at her.

'You go. Go off and enjoy yourselves.' Kiall dismissed Sacha and Mark with an imperious hand. 'Inconsistency, thy name is woman,' he misquoted sarcastically. 'There Sacha goes with Mark McCarthy when she was giving us all hell a few weeks ago about Leon Keppler, who incidently appears to have latched on to Karen.'

'I think you're right.' Ally watched Leon and Karen disappear on to the veranda. 'Shouldn't you give me permission to go about my work?'

'I can promise you I'll wring your neck if I find you giving Fulbrook the slightest encouragement.' Kiall's silver eyes ran over her deliberately.

'And I can promise you a stiff prison sentence. I repeat, I will not be dictated to.'

'Then we're going to have an exceptionally stormy time ahead.'

'My dearest Kiall!' An elderly lady, the wife of a distinguished diplomat, moved through a parting crowd towards them. 'Such a fabluous evening! And you, my dear.' Shrewd, kind eyes looked Ally over. 'Susan tells me you've handled everything. I must congratulate you. It's like the old days when . . . when . . . '

'When Mowana was *en fête*,' Ally helped Lady Henderson out of her predicament. When Kiall's mother was mistress of Mowana had trembled on her lips. Even in that short period she had made an unforgettable impression. 'Will you excuse me, Lady Henderson?' Ally said now. 'I must organise supper for the band.'

'Of course, my dear, of course. What a splendid creature!' The loud voice of the partially deaf woman wafted after her. 'Why don't you snatch her up, Kiall?'

Ally fled.

Susan and Major Dawson won the treasure hunt: a weekend for two at a beautiful Great Barrier Reef island resort.

'You'll have to come, Susan,' Major Dawson laughed. 'I'll take the bungalow next door.'

A waiter backed into Ally, splashing champagne over her bare arm. He wiped it away quickly with a damask napkin, apologising profusely, but Ally's skin felt sticky and she hurried away to her room to wash it off.

She was drying her arm in the adjoining bathroom when she heard the bedroom door open and shut.

'Sacha?' She walked out quickly, a queer prickling on her skin.

'This must be the only way I can see you alone,' Alan Fulbrook smiled at her from the sofa.

'You must be out of your mind,' Ally said icily. 'Get out of my room!'

'Have you forgotten?' His smile was cynical. 'You invited me here.'

'Did I ask you what your game was?' Ally voice dripped contempt. 'Is this some little ploy you've thought up with your mother?'

Alan Fulbrook leaned back against the sofa and put his locked hands behind his head. 'If there's one thing our beloved Kiall has never been able to tolerate, it's infidelity in a woman. Mother and I put our great brains together.'

'You don't have one brain between the two of you,' Ally snapped. 'Aren't you overestimating my friendship with Kiall?'

'I don't think so.' Alan Fulbrook's dark eyes glittered. 'For a man who's been around, I've never seen him the way he is with you. He looks like a man at war with his strong natural instincts. He wants you but he doesn't trust you, and that's the way we're going to undermine you.'

'I do hope you're not going to suggest rape?' Ally said sarcastically. She began to walk to the door. 'I should tell you I've studied karate for years.'

'You'd make a wonderful wrestle!' Alan Fulbrook locked his arms around her waist, and Ally kicked back and brought the high heel of her black satin evening shoe down on his foot.

'You bitch!'

'Like it?' She whirled and picked up a jade sculpture.

'You don't want to do that.' He inched towards her. 'That's valuable.'

'I'm sure my host won't mind.'

'That isn't glass, girlie, that's worth thousands of dollars.'

'Take one step towards me and you'll soon find out. I'm sure Kiall is going to appreciate what you're doing.'

'Of course he is. He'll see it our way. You don't know much about him, do you? He had an exceptionally hard childhood. His old man nearly went crazy when his wife walked out of the door. Of course, she had to. She wasn't the sort of woman, I'm told, who could be ruled with an iron hand. Austin Lancaster set out to embitter his son. Why do you think it's taken him so long to get married, when he could have had his pick of every available socialite in the country? He wants a woman he can trust.'

'Like Karen?'

'You're absolutely right. Put that jade down, Allegra. You look like an avenging goddess with the light on you.'

When it really came to it, she knew she couldn't risk damaging anything so beautiful and valuable. Ally put the sculpture down on the small circular table and looked at him with contempt. 'You're quite a nasty family, aren't you?'

'Not really. I'm only trying to help out my sister.'

'You really believe that?' Ally asked furiously. 'You really think you're helping your sister by trying to compromise me?'

'Well, you're the enemy, aren't you?' Alan returned coolly. 'I have to come to her defence in this matter.'

'In this way?' Ally looked at him incredulously. 'I thought, quite apart from any other consideration, you were a sportsman.'

'Ah, come off it.' For the first time, the good-looking face looked unsure.

'Do you honestly attack women?'

'Who's attacking?' The dark eyes were fixed intensely on Ally. 'You said it yourself, we're only playing games. Not that I really want to, damn it.' He frowned darkly. 'You're the most interesting female I've ever met. But you know it's hard to resist Mother. The only game she knows is winning.'

'You won't win this way,' Ally assured him with the ring of truth. 'Neither will you help your sister. You think about it, really think about it. Karen is Kiall's choice? He wants her? He's determined on marrying her? Just give him enough time?'

'He might have if you hadn't come along to unsettle him,' Alan answered with an angry flash of resentment.

'I have the feeling you don't really believe that.'

'Mother knows best.'

'No, she doesn't, Alan. She doesn't know what's best for you, and she doesn't know what's best for Karen. She should have encouraged Karen to find someone else long ago, not your neighbour. Kiall does not love Karen. Good God, haven't you all got enough pride to face it?'

'He used to care about her . . .' Alan trailed off lamely.

'He still cares about her in some way. As someone he had known all his life. Why do you all want to lose his friendship? Why, for that matter, are you jeopardising your relationship with him? This afternoon you played in his team. It seemed to me you were all having a great time.'

'The best!'

'Say, for instance, Kiall did care about me,' Ally ventured. 'How do you think he'd feel about you if he found you here in my room. Worse, wrestling with me?'

'I must be deranged!'

'That's the first sensible thing you've said.'

'So what now?' Alan looked at her wryly. 'Basically, I'm not a bad guy, but you've no idea how much pressure my mother can exert. She thought Karen would make a great wife for Kiall.'

'But it's all about who does the choosing. Surely you see that? In my opinion, your mother is only traumatising her only daughter. In the same situation, my mother would have made me see the reality of the situation. Isn't love taking care of someone? Why don't you take care of your sister? All this business is affecting her.'

'You're right.' Alan sat down on the arm of the sofa. 'To a certain extent, Dad and I have kept out of this. My mother is only a little lady, but she's very aggressive and assertive. She had reared Karen to believe she was going to marry Kiall Lancaster at some point. Karen was to become mistress of Mowana. That was the high point in our lives.'

'I'm sorry,' Ally said. 'Truly sorry. I understand how it has all happened.'

'Forgive me?' He got up and walked towards her.

'I guess I'll have to.'

'In actual fact, you've put a hole in my sock.' He stared down at his foot. 'Have you really studied karate?'

'Brown belt.'

'Kiss and make up?'

'You're very cheeky, Alan,' she said softly.

'And you're the best. I just didn't know.' He took hold of her arms gently and bent his head, kissing her on the cheek.

'So there they are!' The door burst open and Karen Fulbrook barged in, tiny little muscles twitching all over her face. Kiall stood back in the hallway, his handsome face overshadowed by an anger barely under control. 'I told Kiall she had brought you up here,' she shouted at her brother, 'but he didn't believe me.' She laughed a little wildly. 'Two-timer that she is.'

'Let's get out of here, Karen.' Alan moved rapidly, grasping his sister's arm. 'I've never noticed before, but all this crazy jealously is making you unattractive.'

'What were you doing here?' Kiall asked for the first time, a curious pallor beneath his sun-coppered skin.

Alan shook his head at this point, as though he couldn't think of a suitable explanation.

'He was with her,' Karen muttered violently. 'Women like her need a dozen men in their lives.'

'Why don't you take your sister and go?' Ally suggested firmly.

'That's not satisfactory to me,' Kiall said, his emotions now under control, but replaced by an icy menace.

'Goodbye, Alan,' Ally said.

'This had to do with something my mother thought up,' Alan said, looking at Kiall with a mixture of appeal and panic.

'Alan!' Karen looked up at her brother, glassy-eyed.

'So you do what you're told. A mother's boy,' Kiall said with chilling arrogance.

'Listen, Kiall, I know you want to kill me.'

'So why don't you go?' Ally cried, her voice soaring. 'Get out of here while there's still time.'

'Why don't you let me handle this?' Kiall turned on Ally, his eyes flaring like diamonds.

For answer she rushed towards the door and shielded brother and sister with her body. 'Because I've worked like mad all week to make this a great party. Go, Alan, you idiot!'

'What's going to happen to you?' he asked with real anxiety.

'Nothing. Absolutely nothing,' Ally answered fierily.

'Why did you do this, Alan?' Karen was gasping.

Her brother returned a furious, exasperated, 'Shut up!'

Despite Ally's natural courage, tremors of fear were flickering down her arms. She shut the door firmly after the Fulbrooks and leaned back against it. Her eyes were brilliant with emotion, enormous, and colour poured into her creamy skin. She looked wild, a little strange and incredibly beautiful.

'Do you mean to kill me?' she demanded with a tilted chin.

'I think I'd enjoy it.' Kiall's voice had deepened to a growl.

'You have no confidence in me? Don't turn your head, I'm not letting you off the hook, Kiall Lancaster. Just answer the question. You have no confidence in me? You don't trust me to behave in a decent manner?'

'I just couldn't believe it,' he rasped, 'when Karen came to me saying you and her brother had gone off alone together. To your bedroom.'

'Oh?' Ally put one agitated hand beneath her heavy, silken mane and threw it back from her face. 'You know so little about me, you thought I was going to seduce a complete stranger?'

'It has happened before.'

'You fiend!' Ally saw stars. She looked about wildly for something to throw, her pulse-rate soaring. Even in her righteous anger she avoided the jade statuette, and picked up an ornament of significant size. She had a thirst for blood. Blood!'

She hurled the red lacquer box as hard as she could. Kiall ducked predictably and it crashed into the wall, dislodging the enchanting painting of the little West Highland terrier. It bumped unharmed to the thick Persian rug, where it lay face up.

'Now look what you made me do.' The furious tears blinded Ally's eyes. 'Do you really think I'd tolerate a man who doesn't believe in me? I wouldn't care if I were insane about him. Love is trust. You carry your hang-ups to your dying day if you must. Ruin every good relationship you're offered. Men are like that. They put themselves foremost all the time. Well, not my man!'

'Ally, stop. Please stop.' Kiall brought her upwards like a doll. 'I'll fix the painting.'

Even in her frenzy, her flesh was on fire where he touched her. 'That's all you care about. Paintings, property.' A crazy energy was building up in her.

'I care about a nut like you.' He bent her backwards with his strength.

'I'm the nut, right?' Her breath shuddered.

'You certainly don't know when to stop!'

The way he was holding her left her with no recourse but to stare into his blazing eyes.

'Where you're concerned.' He gathered her savagely against him, though her resistance was intense and passionate. Raw emotion was compelling them, an elemental love-hate. His hand speared into her thick hair, and he brought his mouth down punishingly over hers, enclosing it and storming the moist interior.

The onslaught was so violent that she whimpered, a sound that only served to inflame his hunger.

'My dear God!' He lifted her bodily, and while Ally marvelled at the primitive emotion that raged between them he flung her on the bed, his diamond-hard eyes licking all over her. She sat up frantically, trying to pull the shoe-string strap of her evening dress back on to her shoulder.

He pushed her back on to the bed wordlessly, and she seemed to sink into billowing clouds of dark rapture. She was struggling no longer, but he kept his strong arms clamped on either side of her body, devouring her mouth, then her throat and the exposed swell of her creamy breast.

Such a confusion of emotion raged in Ally, she couldn't call up a word of protest. She was weak and dizzy with desire, so even as his hands slid under her to release the zipper of her dress she arched her back in consent. Her overwhelming need of him drove everything else from her mind. She could not constrain her body's needs.

'Ally, you're crying.' He stopped abruptly, a flame of tenderness dispelling the pagan ruthlessness.

'Am I?' She brought up a shaky hand, stroking her heavy lashes. 'Why shouldn't I? You're breaking my heart.'

'What do you think you're doing to me?' he returned, mockingly ardent. The hand that moved caressingly from the slope of her shoulder to her breast registered the intensity of his desire. 'I'm aching to make love to you. Not these desperate little half-measures. You should know I can't think of anything else. It's unbearable to be with you and not touch you. I'd give my life for you."

Ally lay back against the pillows, staring up at him with an agonised expression.

'Surely you know?' he asked tersely. 'Don't look so shocked. I was bitterly angry with Fulbrook, never you. I was wondering how far I could go without having to answer for a murder charge. I trust you, Ally. I trust you with my life, my happiness, Mowana, the whole package. You're the magic in everything. You've bought me to the point where I can no longer go it alone. Who cares if you know?'

Ally's golden eyes were lit with a strange glow. 'I have to fight to take all this in,' she said slowly. 'You love me?'

'I sure do.' His shapely mouth twisted. 'The first time I laid eyes on you, I felt as if I had been struck by a lightning-bolt. But you were so young, so very young. I thought of you as a gorgeous kid. A wild one. Even then, I thought of you often. You can imagine how I felt when you turned up as Sacha's friend. That day at the airport, my God! It seemed to me like kismet. That, incidentally, is the name of the next Arabian foal. Kismet. For you and me.'

'Kismet,' Ally repeated dreamily. 'What a wonderful word! I think you'll have to pinch me to prove I'm not dreaming.'

'Why don't you let me kiss you instead?' Kiall suggested tenderly. 'You're so good and beautiful and efficient.'

For long moments, rapture unfolded like a giant rose, a powerful passion and tenderness that merged their spirits and fulfilled the complex array of all their deepest, inner-most longings. It was excitement, elation, certainty. A tremendous commitment. This was a very, very important moment in their lives.

'I love you,' Kiall whispered against the shell of her ear. 'Love you. I'd even love you if the party had turned out a dud!'

'But it's marvellous, admit it.' Ally linked her arms behind his head. 'I adore you, do you know that? I hope you never get tired of hearing it.'

'How long is eternity?' Kiall searched her eyes. 'Let's get engaged tonight.'

'Tonight?' Her voice was incredulous. 'I don't think I could take the excitement.'

'Of course you can,' he said vibrantly.

'What about the Fulbrooks?'

'What about them?' His eyebrow lifted. 'Do they deserve our consideration?'

'I suppose not. Mrs Fulbrook might break out in splotches, but this is *our* party. Oh, Kiall!' Ally's heart melted with love. 'I'll make you so happy, I promise. I'll say my prayers every night.'

He laughed gently, lowering his head and tenderly kissing her mouth. 'Marry me, Ally,' he begged.

'As soon as you say.'

'What about tonight? I'm so starved for you.'

She sat up so that their faces were only inches apart, 'Not tonight,' she said firmly, touching a finger to the cleft in his chin. 'I want a big wedding. Do it all right. That's my philosophy. You're never going to forget your radiant bride. When you're ninety and I admit to fifty, you'll still be talking about how I looked that day. I just need six weeks, maybe eight at the outside. Time for all the invitations to go out. There's my dress, my bridesmaids, matron of honour . . . Is that OK?' She had to hold his face as he suddenly lost attention. 'What's the matter?'

'There's something wrong about the wall,' Kiall said frowning.

'There is?' She turned swiftly, following his gaze. 'Let's get this straight. I'm talking about our wedding and you're interested in the wallpaper?'

'It's a safe,' Kiall said, keeping his arm around her and leading her towards it. 'A safe of some sort. It was disguised by the wallpaper and covered by the painting. God knows, it's hung there ever since I can remember.'

'Without dusting?'

'No one would shift it,' he said. 'Keppler didn't get so far. The room was prepared for you, certainly, but no one has ever thought to rearrange the paintings. Except you.'

'So open it,' Ally said, amazed. Even her hands started trembling.

Inside were four green velvet boxes and a parcel of letters secured with a broad band.

'Do you believe that?' she said shakily. 'These things would have belonged to your mother.'

'I think so.' His handsome face, so exultant one moment, had turned sombre.

'Aren't you going to have a look, darling?'

'Not me. You.'

'All right,' Ally said in a low voice. Loving him so much, she was now sharing his old despair, She reached in and drew out the velvet boxes first, going to the circular table and settling them down. 'These can't hurt you. I'll never let anything hurt you.' She opened up the boxes in turn. All contained exquisite jewellery: necklaces, ear-rings, a single magnificent ring of sapphires and rubies. She couldn't speak. The letters were addressed to Mr Austin Lancaster, Mowana Station, North Queensland. There were twenty or more of them. All of them had been opened.

'These are addressed to your father,' Ally finally got out. 'A woman's writing, a flowing, vital hand. I feel in my heart they're from your mother. It's shattering, isn't it?'

He stared at her for a long moment, his thoughts turning to other days. 'That's my mother's jewellery, of course. Her engagement ring. I'd know it anywhere. My father always said she took everything.'

'What else might he have said that was wrong?'

'It's too late now to know.'

'Is it?'

'Yes, it is, Ally,' he said swiftly, his tone metallic. 'I won't have anything spoil tonight.'

'No.' Quietly she returned everything to the safe and Kiall moved to replace the painting. 'Are you sorry this happened?' Ally turned to look into his eyes.

'I think it would have been too much, only you're beside me. I always understood my mother never corresponded with my father. Only through her solicitor.'

'Well, it's clear she wrote to him for years.'

'Leave it now, Ally,' he ordered her quietly. 'I've always found thoughts of the past depressing. All that interests me now is my furture with you.'

Two months later, the society pages of the nation's papers carried a magnificent smiling photograph of Mr and Mrs Kiall Lancaster of Mowana Station as they emerged from the cathedral moments after their wedding. The church ceremony and the first reception were held in Sydney to facilitate travelling arrangements for the four hundred guests. The second reception, the article reported, was to be held on the historic Outback station, before the happy couple left for their honeymoon in the United States.

In the background of many of the photographs that later appeared in the glossy magazines, was the same beautiful, dark-haired woman of mature years. She had to be family because she bore a close resemblance to the groom. In all of them she was smiling brilliantly. The romantics said she had tears of joy in her eyes.

Happiness is within reach, if we only believe and act upon it.

◆ Harlequin Romance®

Coming Next Month

2977 RANSOMED HEART Ann Charlton
Hal Stevens, hired by her wealthy father to protect Stacey,
wastes no time in letting her know he considers her a spoiled
brat and her life-style useless. But Stacey learns that even
heiresses can't have everything they want....

2978 SONG OF LOVE Rachel Elliott
Claire Silver hadn't known Roddy Mackenzie very long—yet
staying in his Scottish castle was just long enough to fall in love
with him. Then suddenly Roddy is treating her as if he thinks
she's using him. Has he had a change of heart?

2979 THE WILD SIDE Diana Hamilton
Hannah should have been on holiday in Morocco. Instead, she
finds herself kidnapped to a snowbound cottage in Norfolk
by a total stranger. And yet Waldo Ross seems to know all
about Hannah.

2980 WITHOUT RAINBOWS Virginia Hart
Penny intends to persuade her father, Lon, to give up his
dangerous obsession with treasure hunting. She *doesn't* intend
to fall in love with Steffan Korda again—especially since he's
financing Lon's next expedition in the Greek islands.

2981 ALIEN MOONLIGHT Kate Kingston
Petra welcomes the temporary job as nanny to three children in
France as an escape from her ex-fiancé's attentions. She hasn't
counted on Adam Herrald, the children's uncle. Sparks fly
whenever they meet. But why does he dislike her?

2982 WHEN THE LOVING STOPPED Jessica Steele
It is entirely Whitney's fault that businessman Sloan
Illingworth's engagement has ended disastrously. It seems only
fair that she should make amends. Expecting her to take his
fiancée's place in his life, however, seems going a bit too far!

Available in May wherever paperback books are sold, or
through Harlequin Reader Service:

In the U.S.
901 Fuhrmann Blvd.
P.O. Box 1397
Buffalo, N.Y. 14240-1397

In Canada
P.O. Box 603
Fort Erie, Ontario
L2A 5X3

Harlequin Superromance

Here are the longer, more involving stories you have been waiting for ... Superromance.

Modern, believable novels of love, full of the complex joys and heartaches of real people.

Intriguing conflicts based on today's constantly changing life-styles.

Four new titles every month.
Available wherever paperbacks are sold.

"GIVE YOUR HEART TO HARLEQUIN" SWEEPSTAKE!

OFFICIAL RULES

NO PURCHASE NECESSARY TO ENTER OR RECEIVE A PRIZE

1. To enter and join the Harlequin Reader Service, rub off the concealment device on all game tickets. This will reveal the values for each Sweepstakes entry number and the number of free books you will receive. Accepting the free books will automatically entitle you to also receive a free bonus gift. If you do not wish to take advantage of our introduction to the Harlequin Reader Service but wish to enter the Sweepstakes only, rub off the concealment device on tickets #1-3 only. To enter, return your entire sheet of tickets. Incomplete and/or inaccurate entries are not eligible for that section or sections of prizes. Not responsible for mutilated or unreadable entries or inadvertent printing errors. Mechanically reproduced entries are null and void.

2. Either way, your Sweepstakes numbers will be compared against the list of winning numbers generated at random by computer. In the event that all prizes are not claimed, random drawings will be held from all entries received from all presentations to award all unclaimed prizes. All cash prizes are payable in U.S. funds. This is in addition to any free, surprise or mystery gifts that might be offered. The following prizes are awarded in this sweepstakes:

(1)	*Grand Prize	$1,000,000	Annuity
(1)	First Prize	$35,000	
(1)	Second Prize	$10,000	
(3)	Third Prize	$5,000	
(10)	Fourth Prize	$1,000	
(25)	Fifth Prize	$500	
(5000)	Sixth Prize	$5	

*The Grand Prize is payable through a $1,000,000 annuity. Winner may elect to receive $25,000 a year for 40 years, totaling up to $1,000,000 without interest, or $350,000 in one cash payment. Winners selected will receive the prizes offered in the Sweepstakes promotion they receive.

Entrants may cancel the Reader Service at any time without cost or obligation to buy (see details in center insert card).

3. Versions of this Sweepstakes with different graphics may appear in other mailings or at retail outlets by Torstar Corp. and its affiliates. This promotion is being conducted under the supervision of Marden-Kane, Inc., an independent judging organization. By entering the Sweepstakes, each entrant accepts and agrees to be bound by these rules and the decisions of the judges, which shall be final and binding. Odds of winning are dependent upon the total number of entries received. Prizes are nontransferable. All entries must be received by March 31, 1990. The drawing will take place on April 30, 1990, at the offices of Marden-Kane, Inc., Lake Success, N.Y.

4. This offer is open to residents of the U.S., Great Britain and Canada, 18 years or older, except employees of Torstar Corp., its affiliates, and subsidiaries, Marden-Kane, Inc. and all other agencies and persons connected with conducting this Sweepstakes. All federal, state and local laws apply. Void wherever prohibited or restricted by law.

5. Winners will be notified by mail and may be required to execute an affidavit of eligibility and release that must be returned within 14 days after notification. Canadian winners will be required to answer a skill-testing question. Winners consent to the use of their name, photograph and/or likeness for advertising and publicity in conjunction with this and similar promotions without additional compensation. One prize per family or household.

6. For a list of our most current major prizewinners, send a stamped, self-addressed envelope to: WINNERS LIST, c/o MARDEN-KANE, INC., P.O. BOX 701, SAYREVILLE, N.J. 08872

LTY-H49

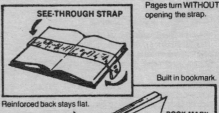